CLASS IS OVER

Frightened children suddenly began to stream around him as they broke for outside. Longarm let them go and kept his attention focused on the four men he spotted at the front of the big, high-ceilinged room. Three of them were dressed in rough range clothes, and they stood in a semicircle around the fourth man, a tall, skinny individual who wore a town suit, a white shirt, and a black bow tie. He had rimless spectacles perched on his long nose, and thin white hair. He didn't look the least bit threatening, but the three cowboys all had their guns out.

"Hold it!" Longarm shouted. His finger was ready on the Colt's trigger. All the kids might not be out of the building yet, and if any of those three gunmen looked like they were going to fire, he was going to drop them without hesitation. He didn't want any more bullets flying around in here than was absolutely necessary.

The man closest to him turned his head and snapped, "Get out of here, you stupid bastard! This is none of your business."

"I make it my business when somebody starts shooting off guns . . ."

TABOR EVANS

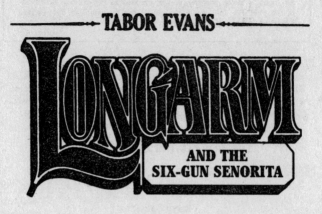

LONGARM

AND THE
SIX-GUN SENORITA

JOVE BOOKS, NEW YORK

This is a work of fiction. Names, characters, places, and incidents are
either the product of the author's imagination or are used fictitiously,
and any resemblance to actual persons, living or dead, business
establishments, events, or locales is entirely coincidental.

LONGARM AND THE SIX-GUN SENORITA

A Jove Book / published by arrangement with
the author

PRINTING HISTORY
Jove edition / July 2001

All rights reserved.
Copyright © 2001 by Penguin Putnam Inc.
This book, or parts thereof, may not be reproduced in any form
without permission.
For information address: The Berkley Publishing Group,
a division of Penguin Putnam Inc.,
375 Hudson Street, New York, New York 10014.

The Penguin Putnam Inc. World Wide Web site address is
www.penguinputnam.com

ISBN: 0-515-13103-2

A JOVE BOOK®
Jove Books are published by The Berkley Publishing Group,
a division of Penguin Putnam Inc.,
375 Hudson Street, New York, New York 10014.
JOVE and the "J" design
are trademarks belonging to Penguin Putnam Inc.

PRINTED IN THE UNITED STATES OF AMERICA

10 9 8 7 6 5 4 3 2 1

Chapter 1

Longarm hadn't seen Julie Cassidy in over a year, not since the last time he'd dropped by her horse ranch in Kansas. So he was a little surprised when he got a note from her asking him to visit her in her hotel room at one of Denver's finest hostelries. He hadn't known she was coming to Denver. When he knocked on the door of her room and she called out to ask who was there, he told her and was instructed to come on in, and not to waste any time about it. He found her lying nude on top of the fancy silk sheets, her tousled blond hair spread out on the pillow around her beautiful face, and that was a little bit of a surprise too.

But a mighty pleasant one.

Now he was the one lying naked on those silk sheets, and Julie was kneeling beside him on the bed with her hand clasping the base of his fully erect manhood and her lips wrapped around the head of the shaft. Longarm stroked her hair as her head bobbed up and down while she sucked him. She was able to swallow less than half of his long, thick pole without gagging, but that was enough. Longarm was awash with sensation, and he knew it wouldn't be long before his climax gripped him.

"I reckon you better climb on, gal," he warned Julie,

1

"unless you want things to wind up right where they are now."

Julie lifted her head and smiled at him, her eyes half shut and shining with lust. She swung a smooth, creamy thigh over him and straddled his hips. His shaft pointed straight up at its target. Julie guided it in as she lowered herself onto him. He went into her easily, since her opening was already soaked with the juices of her own arousal. Her lips parted and she gasped as she hit bottom with his manhood filling her completely.

"Oh, Custis," she said huskily. "I've been missing you so much."

Longarm thrust up into her, sliding smoothly in and out of her velvet grip. He cupped her full breasts in his hands and stroked the hard nipples with his thumbs. "I've missed you too," he said, his voice just as husky with passion as Julie's was.

They had been friends and occasional lovers for a while, ever since Longarm had met her during a case he'd been investigating. Julie raised some of the finest racehorses in the country, in addition to being beautiful and intelligent. Most men would have tried to get a ring on her finger by now, but Longarm knew that wasn't likely to happen. He had packed a badge for Uncle Sam far too long to settle down now, much as he thought he might like to at times.

Julie leaned forward, lying on Longarm's broad chest, which was matted with thick, dark brown hair. As she kissed him, he put his arms around her and reached down to grasp her buttocks. Her hips pumped even harder, thrusting his shaft in and out of her. Their tongues met, fenced with each other, darted hotly around each other's mouth. Finally, gasping again with the need for release, Julie sat up straight and rode him hard and fast for several moments until she cried out, "Now, Custis, give it to me now!"

Longarm was more than ready. He grabbed her hips to steady her and drove up into her as far as he could go, holding himself there as his organ began to throb. His thick white seed boiled out of his balls and up his shaft, exploding into her waiting sheath in spurt after hot spurt. An intense shudder ran through Julie's entire body as Longarm filled her to the brim and then overflowing.

Then she sighed in deep satisfaction and collapsed onto his chest again. Longarm's pole, drenched now, remained firmly embedded inside her. His pulse pounded in his head like a prairie thunderstorm. He put his arms around Julie and held her tightly.

She nuzzled her lips against his neck, then lifted her head and kissed him again, laughing a little as his long-horn mustache tickled her mouth. "I swear, Custis," she said, "I wish we could get together more often."

"So do I," Longarm said honestly. "Our work keeps both of us mighty busy, though."

Julie sighed. "I guess there's no getting around it, is there? Anyway, it's my work that's brought me to Denver. I'm here to deliver a horse to a buyer."

"I'm glad he didn't go to Kansas to pick up the horse then. Otherwise we wouldn't be here like this now."

"That's right." Julie gave him another peck on the lips. "I'm turning over the horse tomorrow, but I think I could manage to stay here in town another few days if you'd like. My foreman can keep the ranch running just fine for a while."

Longarm liked the sound of that. He was about to say as much when somebody knocked lightly on the door. The tapping had a tentative sound to it. Longarm muttered, "Damn!" and looked at Julie. "Was that buyer of yours coming here tonight?"

She shook her head, "No, I wasn't expecting anyone. I don't have any idea who it could be, Custis."

Longarm thought about reaching for his gun. His holster was hung on one of the bedposts so that the butt of the .44 was in easy reach. A man in his line of work always had plenty of enemies to choose from.

But if somebody wanted him dead and had followed him there, chances are the gent would have just busted through the door and started shooting. They wouldn't

3

stand out in the hall and tap on the door like that.

"Marshal? Marshal Long? Are you in there?"

Longarm recognized the voice. It belonged to the clerk from the desk downstairs. The fella had seen him come through the lobby earlier, recognized him, and given him a friendly nod. Longarm had met Julie Cassidy here often enough over the years so that the clerk had probably guessed where he was going.

Longarm didn't like it, but he had to let go of Julie. He rolled to the side, then swung his legs off the bed. Julie was getting up on the other side and reaching for a robe.

Longarm picked up his trousers and yanked them on, none too happy about being disturbed this way. He went to the door, asked, "What is it?" and out of habit stepped to one side. It had been a while since somebody had let loose at him through a door with a shotgun, but such unfriendly things had been known to happen.

"I hate to bother you, Marshal," said the clerk, "but I have an urgent message here for you from Chief Marshal Vail. He says for you to come to his office as soon as possible."

"Now?" said Longarm. "It's a hell of a long time past regular office hours."

"All I know is what the message says, Marshal."

Longarm frowned and said, "Wait a minute. Who delivered this message?"

"A young man who said he was Marshal Vail's secretary."

"Henry," muttered Longarm. He should have known. The pasty-faced gent who played the typewriter in Billy Vail's outer office had a long-standing grudge against Longarm. This was Henry's idea of a practical joke. It had to be. Henry was especially mad at Longarm right now because a couple of days earlier Longarm had paid one of the gals from the Palace Saloon to stuff a pillow under her dress so she'd look like she was in the family way, then wander around the Federal Building for a while asking everybody she saw if they knew where she could find Henry. The look on Henry's face was funny as hell

4

when he heard about it. But Longarm probably should have tried not to laugh, he told himself now. That had been a dead giveaway.

Billy Vail wouldn't call him down to the office in the middle of the night like this. Longarm had to admit that Henry had come up with a pretty good joke, though. For a minute there, he'd believed it.

"Consider the message delivered," Longarm called through the door to the clerk.

"Then you'll be going to Marshal Vail's office?"

"Sure thing." Longarm gestured for Julie to take the robe off. She smiled and shrugged out of the garment, letting it fall to the floor around her feet. She stood there on the other side of the room, gloriously nude, and as Longarm drank in the sight of her, he felt his shaft beginning to harden again. It was going to be a long night, and he was good for several more go-rounds. As he stepped away from the door, he said to the clerk, "Just as soon as I'm finished with my business here."

"What? What was that, Marshal Long?" the clerk asked.

But Longarm ignored the clerk, seeing as how he was already occupied again, and after a while the fella gave up and went away.

Chapter 2

It was after midnight when a hard fist pounded loudly on the door and an angry voice called, "Damn it, Longarm, if you're in there you'd better get this door open pronto!"

Longarm had sort of dozed off with Julie's head resting on his groin after she'd given him a French lesson that seemed to shake the whole world. He lunged up off the bed and caused her to yelp in surprise. She was no more shocked than Longarm himself, though.

The voice yelling in the hall belonged to none other than Chief Marshal Billy Vail himself.

Longarm rolled out of bed, grabbed his pants for the second time tonight, and hustled over to the door. Behind him, Julie dived under the covers, pulling them all the way over her head. Longarm said, "Hold on, Billy," and turned the key in the lock. He opened the door a few inches and peered out into the corridor.

His boss stood there wearing a gray suit, a cream-colored Stetson, and a string tie. Vail's broad face looked a little more pink than usual. "Blast it, Longarm," he snapped, "where the hell have you been?"

"Uh, right here, Billy," Longarm replied cautiously.

"Well, didn't you get my message?" demanded Vail.

"Message?" For a second, Longarm thought about denying that he'd ever heard about any such thing. That wouldn't be fair to the hotel clerk, who had faithfully delivered the message, though, so Longarm went on. "Sure I did, Billy."

"Then why aren't you in my office right now instead of tomcatting around?"

"You mean you meant for me to come to the office tonight?"

Vail gritted his teeth in exasperation. "That's what I told Henry to tell you. He came back to the Federal Building and told me that he had given the message to the clerk here and that the man had promised to deliver it."

"Well, then, I'm sure that's just what Henry did. I reckon I just didn't understand how urgent this matter is." Longarm had no idea what *this matter* was, but it damned well had to be important to drag Billy Vail out of a warm bed at this time of night.

"Get dressed and come down to the office," Vail said. "I'd rather tell you about it there. And I mean *now*."

"Sure, Billy. I'll be right there."

Vail folded his arms across his chest. "Maybe I'll wait downstairs for you, just to be sure."

Longarm started to tell him that wasn't necessary, but he saw the smoldering fires in Vail's eyes and decided not to risk it. He nodded in agreement and said, "I'll be there in two minutes." He shut the door.

As soon as she heard the door close, Julie's head popped out from under the covers. "Two minutes!" she said. "That's not long enough to say a proper good-bye."

"We don't know I'm going anywhere," Longarm told her. "I may be back in half an hour."

Julie shook her head sadly. "I'm not going to count on that. Marshal Vail wouldn't have come here himself if it wasn't something awfully important. You may be leaving town in less than an hour."

That was possible, thought Longarm. Whatever Vail had to say to him, evidently it really was urgent, and not a joke on Henry's part at all. Longarm wished he hadn't miscalculated so badly.

But making mistakes was all part of learning, he told

himself, and although it was more years than he liked to think about since he'd left West-by-God Virginia at the conclusion of the war, he still wasn't too old to learn things.

He dressed hurriedly, leaving off his long underwear and settling for his trousers, shirt, boots, and hat. He draped his vest and coat over his left arm as he leaned over the bed to kiss Julie good-bye. "I'll come back if I can," he promised.

"I know," she sighed. "But if you don't, I'll deliver that horse tomorrow and head back to Kansas. There'll be another time for us."

"Damn right," said Longarm.

Billy Vail was waiting downstairs in the lobby, as he had promised. The clerk who had come upstairs earlier was still on duty. He shot nervous glances toward Longarm as the big lawman strode across the lobby to join Vail. Longarm gave him a quick grin to let him know that he wasn't in trouble.

"Come on," Vail said. He stepped out of the hotel and started walking toward the Federal Building. Longarm had no trouble keeping up with his boss, but the brown tweed trousers he wore were starting to scratch at his privates. He sighed, resigned to the discomfort.

Vail's outer office was deserted. "Where's Henry?" asked Longarm.

"I sent him home after I told him that I'd go find you myself. I didn't see any reason to keep him up all night just because you can't take orders."

Billy had an even bigger burr than usual up his butt tonight, Longarm thought. He kept quiet and followed Vail into the inner office.

When both men were sitting down, Vail behind the big desk and Longarm in the red leather chair in front of it, the chief marshal picked up a piece of paper and held it out. "Read that," he ordered.

Longarm took the paper. It was a telegram from Justice

8

Department headquarters in Washington and was addressed to Vail.

SHIPMENT OF ARMY RIFLES STOLEN IN TEXAS **STOP** MEXICAN BANDITS SUSPECTED **STOP** SEND BEST MAN PRESIDIO SOONEST **STOP** SEE RANGER HORNE **STOP**

Longarm looked up at Vail. "So somebody ran off with a bunch of Army rifles and the War Department asked the Justice Department for help in getting 'em back," he said, filling in the missing pieces of the puzzle.

"That's right. And you see right there it says *soonest*."

"It says *best man* too," Longarm pointed out dryly.

Vail ignored that. He said, "I got another telegram tonight, a private telegram, from the Attorney General. Things are touchy betwixt our government and the Mexican government right now—"

"As usual," muttered Longarm.

"So the Attorney General asked me to see to it that a deputy marshal with diplomatic skills investigates the theft as soon as possible," Vail pressed on.

Longarm sat back in the red leather chair and reached into the pocket of his vest, which was lying across his lap. He took out a cheroot. "I ain't known for being a diplomat, Billy," he said. "I tend to sort of stir things up when I go poking into something."

"I know that. But I figure the best way to keep from straining relations between the U.S. and Mexico is to get those guns back in a hurry so nobody south of the border can use 'em to try to overthrow President Diaz."

Longarm nodded slowly. "I reckon that makes sense. If the rifles are already across the border, though, I'd have to cross the Rio to go after them. The *federales* and *rurales* know me over there and don't much like me."

"Then try not to cross paths with them," Vail advised. "Not that I'm ordering you to cross the border. Not at all."

Longarm grunted. Vail couldn't officially order him to chase those stolen rifles into Mexico; Longarm understood that. If he got his feet wet in the Rio Grande, he'd be on his own.

He glanced at the telegram from the Justice Department again. "The Texas Rangers already have a man there. Why doesn't he go after the rifles?"

"You'll have to take that up with him. He'll give you all the details, I suppose."

"I suppose," Longarm repeated. He tossed the telegram onto Vail's desk. "When's the first train in that direction?"

Vail checked his pocket watch. "One pulls out for El Paso in less than five hours. You'll have to take the stage from there to Presidio. Your travel vouchers and expense money are on Henry's desk."

Longarm nodded and stood up. "I'll do my best, Billy."

"I know you will." Vail's earlier anger had evaporated. "Be careful, Custis," he said. "This could be a rough one. You'd better go back to your place and get a little sleep before you leave. Just don't miss your train."

Longarm grunted noncommittally. He had other plans in mind for the time he had left in Denver.

He might be a little drowsy on the train tomorrow, but at least Julie Cassidy would get a proper good-bye.

Chapter 3

Longarm stifled a yawn, put a cheroot between his teeth, struck a lucifer on the sole of his boot, and set fire to the thin black cigar. He shook the flame out, dropped the sulphur match on the floor of the railroad car, and ground his boot heel on it. He leaned back against the hard bench seat and tipped his flat-crowned, snuff-brown Stetson forward over his eyes. The urge to yawn struck him again. He took the cheroot out of his mouth so he could indulge the urge.

Drowsy wasn't the word for it. He was worn out. Dog tired. During the few hours they'd had left together, Julie Cassidy had done her damnedest to flat out screw him to death.

And Longarm had enjoyed every minute of it.

He smiled to himself as he recalled the way she had taken his balls in her mouth one at a time and rolled them around with her tongue. Then she'd licked his erect shaft from the base to the crown, toyed with the slit in the end of it with her tongue, and nipped gently at him until his climax had shot all over her pretty face. That was an image that would stay in his mind for a long time and keep him warm on cold, lonely nights.

Longarm was half asleep when someone sat down beside him. He lifted his head and looked through slitted eyes at a sweating, heavyset gent in town clothes and a derby hat. The hombre had a sample case on the floor at his feet. A drummer, thought Longarm, and unless the gent was selling Maryland rye, Longarm wasn't the least bit interested in his wares.

"Good morning," the man said. "Mighty early in the day to be starting a trip, isn't it?"

Longarm grunted. He'd been afraid that the drummer was the talkative sort.

"Of course, the early start means I'll get to Santa Fe in plenty of time to make calls on some of my clients," the drummer went on. "You look like a traveling man yourself, friend. What do you deal in?"

"Lead," said Longarm.

"Really? Represent a smelter, do you? I suppose the industrial line is a good one. I've always enjoyed being in ladies' undergarments myself." The man guffawed at the old joke and elbowed Longarm painfully in the ribs.

An underwear salesman. It was even worse than Longarm had suspected. He closed his eyes, tried not to groan, and hoped he wouldn't have to shoot this son of a bitch before they got to Santa Fe.

Thankfully, the drummer left the train when it stopped in New Mexico's territorial capital later that morning. Longarm's next seatmate was a middle-aged rancher who was as taciturn as the drummer had been loquacious. Longarm counted himself lucky and went to sleep. He dozed right through the stop in Albuquerque, and didn't wake up until the train was well on its way to El Paso.

He reached the city named for the famous pass to the north in the late afternoon, checked the schedule at the stage station, then got a hotel room and went in search of some supper. The next stage eastbound toward Presidio on the line that followed El Camino del Rio—the River Road—wouldn't leave until the middle of the next day.

Longarm ate dinner in the hotel dining room, and then spent the evening alone in his room rather than succumbing to the temptations of the raucous border-town nightlife in El Paso. His time with Julie Cassidy was recent enough to take the edge off any need for a woman, and he didn't want to suffer through a hangover the next day on the stage. Riding one of those bouncing, jolting Concords was hard enough when a fella was stone-cold sober and had been for weeks.

The stage left on time the next day, and Longarm was on it. His McClellan saddle, his Winchester, and his war bag were stored in the vehicle's baggage boot. The only other passengers were the same stony-faced rancher who had ridden down on the train with him and a different drummer who was thankfully the quiet type. The three men didn't say a dozen words an hour among them, and that was all right with Longarm.

The stagecoach followed the route of the old Butterfield Overland Mail part of the way, hugging the curves of the Rio Grande, until it reached a junction where two stage roads came together. The Butterfield route angled to the northeast, toward Fort Stockton, which Longarm had visited during another case several months earlier. The road his stage followed continued on to the southeast, still following the river as befitted its name. The heavily cultivated fields along the Rio Grande, dotted by villages of adobe jacales, some of which had been there for hundreds of years, fell behind the stagecoach. The terrain became more rugged. The jagged gray heights of the Chinati Mountains thrust up toward the wide Texas sky.

The stage stopped for the night at a station on the edge of the mountains. The River Road was too steep and winding for the team and coach to travel by night. The stationmaster, a bearded old-timer who lived a lonely existence there on the edge of nowhere, had chili, beans, cornbread, and coffee ready for the travelers. He and the driver talked over the news from El Paso as they sat at a long, rough wooden table, and then the jehu asked, "What's the word from downriver? Heard anything about Mendoza?"

The stationmaster cursed. "That Yaqui breed's lyin'

low right now, thank the Lord. He ain't been on a raid across the border in over a month."

"That's good," the rancher said. "If I didn't have a mighty salty crew, I reckon Mendoza would've tried to clean me out before now."

Longarm grunted and said, "Who's this Mendoza hombre?"

The other four men looked at him in surprise. The stationmaster risked being rude by asking, "Where are you from, mister?"

"Up Colorado way," replied Longarm.

"Oh. Reckon that explains it then."

The rancher leaned forward and said, "Mendoza's a bandit, been raisin' hell on both sides o' the river down in the Big Bend country for nearly a year now. He's half Yaqui Indian and all mean. Most of the time he stays south o' the border, but he crosses ever' now and then and raids some rancho."

"Sounds like a good man to avoid," Longarm commented mildly.

"Damn right," the rancher said.

The stationmaster took a sip of coffee, then went on. "From what I hear, the ones who are really stirrin' up trouble downriver are a bunch called Los Niños de Libertad."

"The Children of Liberty," Longarm said, translating the Spanish phrase without really thinking about it.

The stationmaster looked a little surprised, but he nodded and said, "That's right. They're some sort of revolutionaries who figure to overthrow Diaz. El Presidente has the *rurales* out lookin' for 'em, but so far they ain't had no luck."

"What has this bunch done that's got Diaz so riled up?"

"Well, they raided a couple o' pack trains carryin' silver up from the mines, and they ambushed a patrol of *rurales,* stole their horses and uniforms, and made 'em march back to their post in nothin' but their long underwear. Their *capitán* was mad as blazes about that. They gave one of the soldiers a letter too, sayin' that Diaz's days of oppressin' the Mexican people are numbered. It got passed on to Mexico City, and Diaz hit the roof when he read it."

Longarm said, "Seems to me that a fella who's got the whole Mexican Army at his beck and call shouldn't be that worried about a bunch of ragtag rebels all the way up the hell and gone in Chihuahua."

"Diaz don't like anybody standin' up to him. He's afraid folks'll talk about it and get the idea in their heads that he ain't all-powerful after all. So he's got to crush every spark of revolt, no matter how little."

Longarm nodded. The stationmaster wasn't telling him anything he didn't already know. He was quite familiar with the high-handed, even brutal methods of Presidente Porfirio Diaz. But he hadn't heard of Los Niños de Libertad before, nor of the bandit called Mendoza. He found both bits of news extremely interesting. A gang of revolutionaries or an outlaw gang, either one could surely use some stolen U.S. Army rifles.

He mulled those possibilities over as he went to sleep on the narrow bunk furnished by the stationmaster. He hadn't even reached Presidio yet, and he already had two leads. Maybe when he got there, the Texas Ranger who was supposed to meet him could tell him something else that would put him on the right trail.

Chapter 4

"I didn't ask for your sorry ass to be sent down here, Long, and as far as I'm concerned, you can haul it back up to Denver where you came from!"

Ranger Sam Horne slammed his fist down on the desk to punctuate his angry statement. He glared across at Longarm, who stood there with a puzzled expression on his face.

"Hold on there, old son," Longarm said, forcing himself not to give in to his own anger at being talked to that way. "Let's eat this apple one bite at a time. All I did was tell you my name, and already you're telling me to get out."

"The Rangers don't need any help from you Federal boys. *I* don't need any help. You understand that, Long, or are you dumb as a jackass?"

Longarm looked down at the dusty floor of the one-man Ranger post. He would have dearly loved to put a fist in the middle of Horne's craggy face right about now, but that wouldn't help him find those stolen rifles. He looked up again at Horne and said, "My boss, Chief Marshal Vail, was a Texas Ranger once. I've crossed paths with plenty more Rangers who were good lawmen. Fella named Coffin, for one. We had our differences, but we worked together just fine. Reckon you and I can too, Horne."

Horne snorted. "You reckon wrong."

Longarm was starting to wonder where the hell he'd taken a wrong turn in this case. He had followed instructions to the letter—he'd gotten to Presidio as quickly as he could, and after stashing his gear at the stage station, had come straight here to the Ranger post and introduced himself to Sam Horne. And all he'd gotten for his efforts so far was grief.

Horne was a medium-sized man, several inches shorter than Longarm, who had a brushlike mustache and a face the color of old saddle leather. He was thick-bodied without actually being fat. His office was in a small adobe building not far from the sprawling compound known as Fort Leaton. It wasn't a military fort, but rather a trading post that had been there on the Rio Grande for more than thirty years. Old Ben Leaton, the pioneer who had taken over the original trading post and turned it into a fortress with high, thick adobe walls, had been the dominant personality in the area for many years until his death, watching a good-sized settlement grow up around the fort. His heirs still ran the huge trading post, which served not only the American town of Presidio, but also the town of Ojinaga on the Mexican side of the river.

Longarm made one more attempt at conciliation. "Look, Ranger, I've been riding in a stagecoach all day, going up, down, and around mountains. I'm covered with dust and my rump hurts from sitting in that blasted Concord. So I know you don't want to cause any more grief for a fellow lawman."

"Only lawman that counts for anything in Texas is a Ranger," snapped Horne. "We've already got a man on the trail of those stolen guns. Ranger name of Jack Ralston from San Antonio. Nobody in these parts knows him, so he's working undercover, poking around on the other side of the border and pretending to be a prospector. When we get those rifles back, we'll let the Army know."

"The Army asked for help," Longarm pointed out. "That's why my boss got orders from Washington to send a man down here."

Horne shook his head stubbornly. "You'd just be in the way. Go home, Marshal."

Longarm threw up his hands in disgust. "Where's the telegraph office? If you want me out of your hair so bad, Horne, I reckon I'll try to oblige you, but the order has to come from Billy Vail."

"Closest telegraph office is at Fort Stockton. You can be there in two days. . . ." Horne paused, then added with a smirk, "By stagecoach."

Longarm looked down at the floor again. He'd had enough, and he was gathering himself to light into Horne, first verbally, and then with fists if that was the way the arrogant bastard wanted it. But before he could say anything, the door of the office opened behind him, and a woman's voice said, "Ranger Horne, Mr. Akin and I were wondering if you found out who stole—oh, I didn't realize you already had a visitor."

Drawn by the husky beauty of the voice, Longarm turned and saw a young woman standing in the doorway, one hand lifted to push back the thick mass of raven-black curls that threatened to spill in front of her face. She wore a somber gray dress that looked totally out of place on her. She would have been more at home, thought Longarm, in a long, brightly embroidered skirt and a peasant blouse cut low enough in front for those full breasts to spill halfway out, instead of straining at the fabric of the dress. Her smooth skin was just a little darker than honey, and her dark eyes were bold as they looked at Longarm, returning his scrutiny.

Horne's voice sounded annoyed as he said, "Don't worry about that, Señorita Gonzalez. This hombre was just leaving, and he doesn't have any business here anyway. I haven't found out anything else about your goats, but when I do, I'll sure let you know."

"Thank you, Ranger," the young woman murmured. "The children miss the milk. We will buy more goats if we have to, but as you know, the school does not have much money."

"Yes, ma'am. I'm still looking into it, I promise you."

"Thank you." The woman looked at Longarm again and nodded. *"Señor."*

Longarm tugged on the brim of his Stetson and said, "Ma'am."

She turned and walked out of the office. The view from the rear was almost as good as the one from the front, thought Longarm. He turned back to the desk and asked, "Who was that?"

"What business is it of yours?" grated Horne.

"Just curious. She's a mighty fine-looking young woman. Speaks English good too."

"She ought to, she's a teacher. Runs a school here with some Yankee fella from back east somewhere." Horne got to his feet. "But you don't have to worry about that, Long, because you ain't goin' to be here long enough to make his acquaintance."

"We'll see," Longarm said. "Now that I'm here, I might just decide to stay awhile, take some time off." He started toward the door, then added over his shoulder, "Who knows, maybe I can find out who stole Señorita Gonzalez's goats."

"You just stay away from Señorita Gonzalez."

Longarm didn't say any more. He left Horne there fuming and went over to the trading post, which was also the main saloon in town. He needed a drink to wash the bad taste of his encounter with the Texas Ranger out of his mouth.

The large, thick wooden gates in the outer wall of the compound were open, and wagons were rolling in and out of the place. Fort Leaton did a booming business, seeing as how Presidio was the main river crossing between El Paso and Del Rio. Longarm strolled across the open ground between the wall and the huge adobe building where the trading post and saloon were located. Several men lounged in cane-bottomed chairs on the front porch, some of them American, some Mexican. Longarm stepped up onto the porch, nodded pleasantly to the men, and stepped through the open double doors into the shadowy interior of the building. The coolness inside was a welcome relief from the blazing heat of the late afternoon sun. In the summer like this, Presidio had to be the hottest place in the state of Texas, he thought.

A long bar ran down the right side of the room. Instead of the usual mirror, red and green chilies hung on the wall behind the bar. A heavyset Mexican man with plenty of gray shot through his thick black hair was tending bar. He smiled at Longarm and asked, "What'll you have, amigo?"

"Wouldn't happen to have any Maryland rye, would you?"

The bartender reached for a bottle. "Tom Moore be all right?"

Longarm grinned broadly. "You must be a saint, because you're about to bring relief to this thirsty traveler."

The bartender put a glass on the bar and splashed whiskey from the bottle into it, saying "Two bits." Longarm slid a silver dollar across the hardwood, picked up the glass, and threw back the drink. He motioned for the bartender to refill the glass.

"Came in on the stage, didn't you?" asked the bartender as he tipped up the bottle.

"Yep." Longarm took his time with this one, savoring the smoky flavor of the rye.

"Saw you go into the Ranger post. If you want, you can tell me to go to hell, but I'm curious about your business with Horne, mister."

Longarm licked his lips and set the empty glass on the bar. An idea suddenly sprang into his mind, and he said, "I'm looking for somebody. Thought the Ranger might be able to help."

"Looking for somebody, eh? Who might that be? I see just about everybody who comes through Presidio."

"Fella called Jack Ralston," Longarm said, pulling the name out of his memories of his talk with Horne and hoping that since Ralston wasn't from these parts, he hadn't bothered to use a false name. "He's my brother."

There was a step beside him, and suddenly, a small hand gripped his arm hard. "Jack? Jack is your brother?"

Startled, Longarm turned his head and found himself looking into the beautiful dark eyes of Señorita Gonzalez.

Chapter 5

As Longarm looked at her in surprise, Señorita Gonzalez
gave a little gasp, released his arm, and took a step back.
"Oh! I . . . I did not mean to . . . you must excuse me,
senor—"

"That's quite all right, ma'am," Longarm told her. "A
lady as pretty as you can grab hold of me any time you
want."

The honey-tinged skin of her face took on a faint reddish hue as she blushed. Her chin tipped up defiantly, and
she said, "I heard you mention Jack Ralston. You said
you are his brother, no?"

This gal obviously knew Ralston, thought Longarm, but
not well enough to realize that he wasn't really the
Ranger's brother. Longarm nodded and said, "That's
right. Name's Custis Ralston."

"You are from San Antonio too?"

"Nope, Denver. But Jack wrote to me and asked me to
pay him a visit down here."

Again, Señorita Gonzalez reached out, as if she wanted
to take hold of Longarm's arm, but she stopped herself
this time. "When?" she asked tightly. "When did Jack
write to you?"

The urgency in her voice told Longarm that something

21

was wrong. Being deliberately vague, he said, "Oh, it's been a good while back . . ."

"Because he has been missing for several weeks now. Surely you knew."

Longarm let his eyes go wide with surprise. "Missing?" he exclaimed. "My brother is missing?"

He wasn't exactly sure why he had told the bartender the lie about being Ralston's brother; he supposed it was for a mixture of reasons. For one thing, he wanted to operate undercover as he carried on his investigation of the stolen rifles, and claiming to be Ralston's brother would give him a legitimate reason for being there in Presidio. Also, he knew that such a maneuver was bound to get under the skin of Ranger Sam Horne, and anything that would annoy Horne sounded good to Longarm at this point. But now it appeared that the masquerade might be paying some unexpected dividends. Señorita Gonzalez's reaction told him there was maybe more to the story than he knew.

Those thoughts flashed through Longarm's brain as the bartender placed his hands flat on the bar and said, "It is true, *señor,* I am sorry to say. Your brother, he went across the border to look for gold and silver, and he has not come back."

The young woman glanced across the bar at him and then said to Longarm, "My brother and I are very worried about Jack. He was our friend."

So Señorita Gonzalez and the bartender were brother and sister. Longarm wouldn't have suspected that, since the bartender looked old enough to be her father. They must have come from a big family, with the bartender being the oldest and the young woman the baby of the family.

"Well, of course you're worried," said Longarm, frowning. "I am too. Ranger Horne didn't tell me anything about Jack being missing. I'm going to have to go back over there and have another talk with him."

Horne was going to love that, Longarm thought, suppressing a grin.

"I will go with you," declared Señorita Gonzalez. She linked arms with him, so that his left arm brushed the swell of her right breast for a second. "By the way, we have not been properly introduced. I am Silvia Gonzalez, and this is my brother Stanley."

Longarm glanced at the bartender. "Stanley?"

The man shrugged his broad shoulders. "It was the name of the padre at the mission here when I was born. My parents admired him very much."

"I'm pleased to make your acquaintance, Stanley," Longarm said. "And you too, Señorita Gonzalez."

She was impatient. "Come, we will see the Ranger again."

When they reached Horne's office, Silvia went in first, and Horne looked up in annoyance from his desk. "I told you just a little while ago—" Then he stopped as he saw Longarm. "What are you doin' back here?"

Longarm was glad Horne hadn't called him by name. He wanted to continue his pose as Ralston's brother for as long as possible.

Before he could speak, Silvia said in an accusing tone, "Señor Ralston says you did not tell him his brother is missing, Ranger Horne."

"Brother?" Horne exclaimed in surprise.

"That's right," Longarm said quickly in a loud, angry voice. "I came to you and asked you for help in locating my brother Jack, and all you told me was that you hadn't seen him lately. You didn't tell me he had disappeared!"

Horne was gaping at him. Seeing the Ranger struck speechless was pleasurable, but Longarm knew it might not last. Horne had no real reason to play along with him on this.

Horne closed his mouth, and then a moment later, to Longarm's surprise, he growled, "Sorry, Ralston. I reckon I should have told you the truth. Your brother went over the border a few weeks ago, and nobody's seen him since." Horne paused, but before Longarm could say anything, he went on. "Still, you'd better do like I told you and go back where you came from. I've sent word to the

23

Mexican government, and the *rurales* are looking for your brother. One missing man is enough, so on my authority as a Texas Ranger, I forbid you to cross the border and go looking for him yourself."

Son of a bitch, thought Longarm. Horne didn't look like he was smart enough to have turned the tables so neatly, but that was exactly what he had done. Longarm had willingly given up any authority he might have as a Federal lawman by posing as an ordinary civilian. The Ranger, who should have been an ally, was turning out to be a dangerous adversary instead.

"But Ranger Horne," Silvia Gonzalez said, "surely you can understand how worried and upset Señor Ralston is by this news."

Horne shrugged again. "Sure. But Señor Ralston is a civilian. He has to leave this to the law."

Longarm felt his teeth grinding together, and forced himself to unclench his jaw. "You'll keep me informed?" he asked tightly.

"Of course," said Horne. "As long as you're here in Presidio. But like I said, there's really nothing you can do, so you might as well go home."

"We'll see," snapped Longarm. He turned to leave the office. Silvia took his arm again and went with him.

Once they were outside, she said, "Ranger Horne is really a good man. You must pardon his manner."

"But what's he doing to find my brother?" Longarm asked. Silvia obviously knew quite a bit about what went on around here, he thought. He might as well get what information he could from her, and besides, it was nice having her walking alongside him like this, her arm linked with his.

"Like he said, he has sent word to the *rurales*. He cannot cross the border himself, you know. That would be illegal. But he knows people too, in some of the villages across the river, and he has sent word to them as well to watch for any sign of your brother." Silvia paused and shook her head. "Poor Jack."

"Why do you say that?"

"I am afraid—" Her voice caught for a second. "I am afraid something has happened to him."

Suddenly, Longarm realized that Silvia Gonzalez had really liked this Jack Ralston. There might have even been a romance between the two of them, he thought. But evidently Ralston had kept his real identity a secret from her, as he should have. Silvia seemed to have no idea that the missing man was really a Texas Ranger.

She sighed. "There is nothing we can do right now, I suppose. Why don't you come with me to the school, Señor Ralston? I must speak with Señor Akin, the man who runs it, and then you will come home and have supper with my brother and me."

"I'm much obliged for the invite, but I don't want to intrude—"

Silvia squeezed his arm. "It will be no intrusion. It is the least we can do for you after you have come all this way only to find that your brother is not here."

"Well, then, I accept." Until he figured out exactly what he was going to do, Longarm wasn't going to turn down the chance to spend more time with a gal as good-looking and friendly as Silvia Gonzalez.

The river was nearby, running strongly at this point because about a mile upstream the Rio Conchos flowed out of Mexico and joined the Rio Grande, adding its water to that of the border river. Longarm saw that they were heading for a large adobe building that reminded him somewhat of a church, only there was no cross and no bell tower on it. That had to be the school, Longarm was thinking, when he suddenly heard the flat crack of a gunshot from inside the building.

Chapter 6

"Dios mio!" Silvia cried. "What—"

Inside the school, children began to scream. Two more shots blasted. Longarm tore loose from Silvia's grip on his arm and ran toward the building. He reached over and yanked the Colt from the cross-draw rig on his left hip as he approached the double doors that stood open in the late afternoon heat.

Silvia ran behind him. He motioned for her to stay back, hoping she would obey but doubting that she would. As a teacher, she would be worried about her charges inside the school.

Longarm slowed as he came to the doors. There had been only the three shots from inside, but that didn't mean the danger was over. The kids in the building were still screaming and crying. Longarm went through the doorway at an angle, his revolver leveled and ready.

Frightened children suddenly began to stream around him as they broke for outside. Longarm let them go and kept his attention focused on the four men he spotted at the front of the big, high-ceilinged room. Three of them were dressed in rough range clothes, and they stood in a semicircle around the fourth man, a tall, skinny individual who wore a town suit, a white shirt, and a black bow tie. He had rimless spectacles perched on his long nose, and

26

thin white hair. He didn't look the least bit threatening, but the three cowboys all had their guns out.

"Hold it!" Longarm shouted. His finger was ready on the Colt's trigger. All the kids might not be out of the building yet, and if any of those three gunmen looked like they were going to fire, he was going to drop them without hesitation. He didn't want any more bullets flying around in here than was absolutely necessary.

The man closest to him turned his head and snapped, "Get out of here, you stupid bastard! This is none of your business."

"I make it my business when somebody starts shooting off guns around younkers," Longarm said in an equally hard voice. "Drop those hoglegs . . . *now!*"

The elderly, birdlike hombre held out his hands toward Longarm. "Please, sir!" he said. "Put your weapon away. This is a place of learning, not of violence."

"You better tell that to these other fellas, mister," said Longarm. "They were the ones doing the shooting."

"Benjamin!" The cry came from Silvia Gonzalez, who rushed into the building just as Longarm had suspected she would. "Benjamin, are you all right?"

"I'm fine, Silvia," the elderly man replied. "Please, you should leave now while I talk to Mr. Calhorn and his friends."

"Didn't sound like talking was what they had in mind," Longarm pointed out. He was getting impatient with this stand-off and wished he could identify himself as a lawman. That might put an end to it. But he wanted to preserve his pose as Jack Ralston's brother if possible, so he decided to wait a little longer.

The gunman who had spoken before said, "Look, mister, we don't want any trouble with you. Our business is with the teacher here."

"Teacher?" Silvia repeated. She moved past Longarm before he could stop her. "Benjamin is not the only teacher in this school. I too am a teacher. Will you wave your guns at me and threaten me too?"

"Damn it," Longarm muttered under his breath. Silvia

27

had plowed right into his line of fire. She was between him and the three gunmen now.

But faced with an angry, defiant woman coming at them, the men reacted as most men would. They got sheepish looks on their faces and started mumbling, and the guns they were holding drooped toward the floor. The spokesman snarled at his companions, "Put those guns away, blast it!" and jammed his own revolver in its holster. He tugged on the brim of his hat and went on. "We're sorry, Miss Silvia—"

"Get out!" she told them. "You have no right to be here. Take your guns and leave!"

The three men started sidling away. Silvia was an impressive sight as she stood there, hands planted on her hips, her eyes flashing fire, and her bosom heaving in the gray dress. Longarm probably would have backed off too if she had been looking at him like that.

He lowered his own Colt but didn't holster it. He realized he was in an aisle between the rows of desks that filled the room, so he moved aside to give Calhorn and his partners plenty of room. They stalked past him, glaring at him, and Calhorn—if that was indeed the spokesman's name—paused for a second to say, "We'll take this up another time, mister."

"Any time you want, old son," Longarm told him.

The three men strode out of the building. The elderly man stepped forward, one hand lifted in concern. "The children," he said. "Are they still outside?"

Silvia shook her head. "I told them all to run home as fast as they could and not come back until tomorrow morning. Don't worry, Benjamin, they're safe."

The man closed his eyes and sighed in relief. "Thank God none of them were hurt."

Longarm holstered his Colt and walked on up the aisle to join Silvia and the old man. "What in blazes was going on here?" he asked. "Who were those hombres?"

"Art Calhorn is the foreman for Gil Hoskins," the man explained. "The other two ride for Hoskins as well."

28

"Who's Hoskins?"

Silvia said, "He owns the biggest ranch in this area on the American side of the river."

Longarm thought back to his companion on the stagecoach ride and, before that, on the train. "Would Hoskins happen to be a tall gent with silver hair who doesn't talk much?"

"That sounds like him," said the old man. "Do you know him?"

"I've met him," Longarm said. "But I don't know how come his men would have a grudge against you."

The old man drew himself up straighter, which made him look less like an ungainly bird. "Silvia and I are trying to bring an education to the children of this region. We teach any who want to come, no matter how poor their parents might be. There are some people who think this is a mistake."

"Like Calhorn and his pards." Longarm's words were a statement, not a question.

"Most of the ranchers would prefer that my people remain poor and ignorant," said Silvia. "According to men like Señor Hoskins, they make better workers that way."

Longarm weighed that and nodded slowly in understanding. "Don't fill poor folks' heads with too many ideas."

"Exactly."

"So Calhorn and his cronies come in here and wave guns and shoot at . . . at my feet and frighten the children," said the old man. "While I don't approve of meeting violence with violence, I *am* grateful for your assistance, sir." He held out his hand. "I'm Benjamin Akin, the headmaster of this school."

"Custis Ralston," Longarm replied as he shook Akin's hand, remembering to use the phony name.

Akin's bushy white eyebrows rose in surprise. "Ralston? Any relation to—"

"Señor Ralston is Jack's brother," Silvia explained. "He has come to Presidio to search for him."

Akin pumped Longarm's hand harder. "Then I wish

you all the luck in the world, Mr. Ralston. Your brother seemed like a fine young man."

"Thank you," Longarm said. "I'm sure Jack will turn up. He was always able to take care of himself."

Longarm wasn't sure of any such thing, but he figured a missing man's brother would try to remain optimistic. As a lawman, he had a pretty good idea what had happened to Jack Ralston. The vanished Ranger probably had found what he was looking for, and the discovery had gotten him a bullet in the head and a shallow grave in the Chihuahuan desert. Either that or he'd been left for the *zopilotes* to pick his bones clean.

Longarm continued. "I'm hoping, though, that you'll tell me everything you can about the time Jack spent here, where he went and what he did. Maybe we can think of something that will help Ranger Horne find him."

Benjamin Akin snorted, and Longarm figured it was a sound of contempt directed at Sam Horne. Akin confirmed that guess by saying, "Ranger Horne is not the most zealous of lawmen. A few days ago, someone stole the goats we keep here to provide milk for the children, as well as to provide funds for the school, and the Ranger has not been able to locate them."

"It's a big country," Longarm said with a shrug. "Easy for some goats to disappear."

Silvia said, "Like Jack disappeared?"

Longarm frowned. He hadn't considered the possibility that there might be a connection between a missing Ranger and some stolen goats. Now that he thought about it, he still didn't see any way the two mysteries could be related. But it was becoming clear to him that things in Presidio had a habit of vanishing, and that was mighty strange.

"I don't know," he said to Silvia. "I don't intend to go back to Colorado until I find out what happened to Jack, though."

That much, at least, was true.

"I hope you do," Silvia said, then turned to Akin. "Benjamin, you must come to supper tonight. Señor Ralston has already said he would eat with us."

"Of course," Akin replied without hesitation. "It would be my pleasure. Just let me prepare a bit for tomorrow's lesson."

With that, he turned to a large slate board at the front of the room and picked up a piece of chalk from his desk to write some words on the board. Akin's printing was a little shaky, but Longarm had no trouble reading what he wrote there.

The Sons of Liberty.

Chapter 7

Longarm stared at the words for a moment, remembering how the old geezer who ran the stagecoach station had spoken of Los Niños de Libertad—the Children of Liberty. What Benjamin Akin had just written on the board was remarkably similar to the name of the revolutionary group that might have stolen those missing Army rifles.

Akin and Silvia noticed his interest, and Akin asked, "What's wrong, Mr. Ralston? Haven't you heard of the Sons of Liberty?"

Longarm ran his thumbnail along the line of his jaw as he said, "Well, I don't know...."

"We're studying the American Revolution, and tomorrow I plan to tell the children all about the Boston Tea Party," Akin continued.

Longarm relaxed. "The Sons of Liberty," he said. "Sure. Old Sam Adams and his bunch."

Akin smiled. "Exactly. I want the children to understand how a small group of men, meeting together largely in secret, were able to fan the flames of rebellion until an entire nation rose up and threw off the shackles of oppression."

The old man's voice had grown stronger as he spoke, until he finished with a ringing sound that would stir the blood of just about anybody who had an ounce of patriotism. Akin sounded a little like a zealot himself, thought Longarm.

Silvia was nodding, caught up in what Akin had said. *"Sí,"* she said. "It is a wonderful story. Very inspiring, especially the way Benjamin tells it."

"The inspiration is in the history, my dear, not in anything that I say or do," Akin said with a smile.

Longarm said, "Well, I reckon it's a good thing you're teaching these youngsters about it, Mr. Akin. All the way down here on the border, they probably don't hear much about the history of their country."

"Many of our students cross the river from Ojinaga every day, Mr. Ralston," Akin replied. "But history can always be instructive, whether it concerns one's own country or not."

"Yep," Longarm agreed.

The three of them left the school. Akin carefully closed the doors behind them to keep out the dust. Together, they walked along the road that followed the river.

Akin said, "I suppose I like to teach about the American Revolution because I'm from the part of the country where it took place, you know. New England, that is. Massachusetts, to be precise."

Longarm had the feeling Benjamin Akin was always precise.

"So I've been able to walk the same ground where many of our bravest patriots walked," Akin went on. "Adams, Jefferson, Franklin, Nathan Hale, Daniel and Quincy Reed, Thomas Paine . . . I've studied them all. My father fought in the Revolution, you know."

"Is that so?" said Longarm. He had the feeling that once Akin got wound up like this, it would be difficult to stop him.

"Yes, indeed. He was quite the hero."

"You must be proud of him."

"Of course."

Silvia slipped her arm through Akin's. "And I am proud of you, Benjamin. You bring more than learning to our children. You also bring hope."

33

"Well, I do my best," Akin said humbly, and Longarm sensed that it wasn't false modesty on the part of the schoolmaster.

When Silvia had first mentioned Akin, back in Sam Horne's office, Longarm had wondered if there was anything romantic between them, just as he had wondered about Silvia and Jack Ralston. Now that he had met Akin, he knew that wasn't the case. Silvia simply admired the old man and regarded him with the same affection as she would have a favorite uncle. Longarm found himself being glad about that. He didn't know if he would be around Presidio long enough to even steal a kiss from Silvia Gonzalez, but if the opportunity came up, he wouldn't mind. She was truly a beautiful young woman.

Art Calhorn was well aware of that fact too, Longarm realized as he recalled how the man had looked at Silvia. Calhorn and his pards had come to the school to hooraw Akin, but that didn't mean the ranch foreman couldn't also be interested in Akin's lovely young assistant. Suddenly, Longarm found himself wondering if Calhorn's interest in Silvia could have had anything to do with Jack Ralston's disappearance. If Calhorn wanted Silvia for himself, and if he regarded Ralston as a threat to that ambition, it was possible Calhorn could have done something to get Ralston out of the way. . . .

Longarm frowned. The simplest cases had a habit of getting complicated when he started poking around in them. For tonight, he decided, he was just going to enjoy having supper with Silvia, her brother, and Benjamin Akin. If he found out anything that would help his investigation, so much the better.

Like most of the other buildings in Presidio, Silvia's home was made of adobe. It was small but nice, with a roof of red clay tiles rather than the plain, flat roof that was common on the other houses. The front yard was adorned with a carefully tended cactus garden. The thick walls kept out most of the heat of the day, so it was refreshingly cool inside. The floor was stone and had thick rugs spread around on it. The furniture was plain but comfortable. Evidently, Silvia and her brother lived there alone, and Longarm wondered about the rest of the family.

"Stanley will be home soon," Silvia said. "I will start supper." She left Longarm and Akin in the combination sitting room and dining room and went into the kitchen.

Akin sat down in a cane-bottomed armchair near the fireplace, which was cold at this time of year, and asked, "Where are you from, Mr. Ralston?"

"Denver," Longarm answered.

"Originally?"

Longarm hesitated. He didn't know what story Jack Ralston might have told to the people of Presidio. He couldn't very well tell the truth—that he was from West-by-God Virginia—when Ralston might have said that he grew up somewhere else. Instead, Longarm chuckled and said, "All over really. Been drifting so long it doesn't seem like I'm from any place in particular."

"What's your line of work?"

Ralston had been pretending to be a prospector. That was good enough for him too, Longarm decided. "Mining, most of the time. But I cowboyed some when I was young."

Akin nodded. "A life of glorious freedom, I imagine."

Yeah, thought Longarm, cowboys were free to eat dust and freeze in the winter and burn up in the summer and get stove up from years in the saddle. Akin might know a lot about history, but obviously he wasn't an expert on the West.

The front door opened, and Stanley Gonzalez came into the room. He was expecting Longarm to be there, and he didn't look surprised to see the schoolmaster as well. "*Buenas tardes*, Señor Akin," he said. A frown appeared on his face. "I heard talk that there was trouble at the school."

Akin nodded. "Yes, but it ended peacefully, thank goodness. Mr. Ralston here sent Art Calhorn and his cronies packing."

Stanley grimaced. "That Calhorn is a bad one. I wish he had never seen Silvia."

Stanley's statement seemed to confirm Longarm's guess that Art Calhorn was interested in Silvia. Longarm remembered Gil Hoskins's comments at the stage station about his crew being a salty one. In this rugged land, ranch hands had to be hard and tough. Calhorn and the rest of the bunch might be more than that, though.

Akin waved off Stanley's comment. "Men like Gil Hoskins and Art Calhorn just don't want any progress to invade their world. They don't like having their hierarchy threatened." The schoolmaster leaned forward and seemed about to go on with his pronouncements, but he was interrupted by Silvia's entrance. The spicy aromas of beans and onions and peppers followed her from the kitchen.

"Stanley, open a bottle of wine," she said. "We have guests tonight." She came over to Longarm and laid a hand on his arm. "Perhaps someday, you and your brother will both be able to share a bottle of wine and a meal with us, Señor Ralston."

Longarm nodded and said, "I hope so."

But he didn't believe that would ever happen. Not for one second. He was already convinced that Jack Ralston was dead.

Chapter 8

The food tasted every bit as good as it smelled. The four of them sat around a heavy, rough-hewn table and ate tamales, stew, and a mixture of beans, peppers, and onions rolled up in tortillas, washing everything down with a robust wine. Longarm ate heartily, thoroughly enjoying the meal.

When they were finished, Akin patted his stomach and said, "I'm too old for such spicy food, Silvia, but it was wonderful."

"Gracias," she said with a smile.

"Mighty fine, ma'am," Longarm told her. "The best I've had in a long time."

Silvia laughed. "You are quick with the smiles and the compliments, Señor Ralston. It must run in the family."

"Jack always was a silver-tongued devil," Longarm ventured. He thought it was a safe enough comment to make.

It brought an answering laugh from Silvia. "Yes, he is," she said. "That is one reason I miss him so."

Longarm wondered what the other reasons were, and hoped that Silvia wasn't going to be hurt too much if the news about Jack Ralston's disappearance turned out to be bad, as Longarm suspected it would.

Dusk had settled down over the border country as they

ate. Stanley got up and lit several candles, and Silvia cleared off the table and went back into the kitchen. Stanley, Akin, and Longarm pulled up armchairs and sat around the fireplace. Stanley and Akin took out pipes and got them going, while Longarm lit one of his cheroots.

It was time to do some more poking around, Longarm decided. He blew out a cloud of smoke from the cheroot and said, "I've heard that things are a mite unsettled below the border. There are supposed to be outlaws and revolutionaries in the area."

Stanley grunted. "There are always outlaws."

"And revolution is always with us as well," said Akin. "Why are you interested in such things, Mr. Ralston?"

"Well, my brother's down there somewhere," Longarm said. "I got to worrying that he ran across Mendoza or that bunch called Los Niños de Libertad, and something might have happened to him."

Stony silence from both men greeted his words.

Longarm looked back and forth between Akin and Stanley. The schoolmaster's lips were pursed in disapproval, while Stanley simply sat there stolidly, his broad face expressionless.

"I say something wrong?" asked Longarm.

"Where did you hear about Los Niños de Libertad?" Akin asked in return.

Longarm shrugged. "Fella at the stagecoach station back up the line said something about it last night."

Akin shook his head and said, "Rumors. Hearsay. Gossip. People can't wait to repeat the things they hear, whether there is any truth to them or not."

"Are you saying there's *not* a gang of revolutionaries who call themselves that?"

Akin leaned forward and gestured with his pipe. "That is exactly what I'm saying, Mr. Ralston. It's all just gossip."

Longarm let his voice sound dubious as he said, "I don't know. That gent seemed mighty sure about it. . . ."

"I assure you, if there *was* such a group, we would have heard about it," said Akin. "Wouldn't we, Stanley?"

"*Sí*, Señor Akin," Stanley agreed. "The stories, they are stories only."

"Well, what about that outlaw called Mendoza?"

Again, Akin grimaced. "Unfortunately," he said, "that fellow is all too real."

Now Stanley nodded and looked more enthusiastic. "Many people have seen Mendoza," he said. "And many people are afraid of Mendoza. He raids the villages in the mountains and the farms in the valleys. He hates Americans, but he hates his own countrymen as well. It is the Yaqui blood in him."

Longarm didn't doubt that. The Yaquis were a standoffish bunch of Indians, but they were also some of the most ruthless. And they had no use for anybody who *wasn't* a Yaqui.

"So I'm right to worry about my brother running into him?"

Akin nodded solemnly. "I hate to say it, but yes." He lowered his voice. "We try not to speak of it around Silvia, but there is a definite possibility poor Jack ran afoul of Mendoza."

"Then it would . . . hurt her . . . if something had happened to him?"

"Of course. They were good friends."

Stanley grunted. "More than that perhaps."

Akin frowned at him and said, "There's no call for that kind of talk, Stanley. Silvia is a fine, decent young woman."

"She is my sister, what else could she be but fine and decent? But I have eyes in my head to see, and what I saw was a man and a woman who might have been more to each other than friends."

"Well . . ." Akin shrugged. "Perhaps. But I see no reason not to hope for the best. Our pessimism must seem terrible to Mr. Ralston here."

Longarm shook his head. "You're just being realistic. I know this is a hard country. Things happen to folks down here along the border, and sometimes there's not a damned thing you can do about it."

They might have said more, but Silvia returned from the kitchen at that moment. Longarm noticed that she had loosened the collar of her dress so that more of her throat was revealed. And it was a fine throat too, he noted. The skin there was just as tanned as her face, so she couldn't wear those high-collared getups all the time. That thought made him visualize her in a peasant blouse again, and that was a mighty distracting image.

She smiled at the three men and said, "You have solved all the problems of the world while I was in the kitchen, no?"

Akin laughed. "Hardly, my dear. I suspect we haven't solved anything."

"But it was a pleasant talk anyway," said Longarm. "I'm much obliged for the hospitality. Reckon I'd better get back and get a room at the hotel."

"I will see you out," Silvia murmured.

Longarm nodded to Akin and Stanley. "Good night."

Both men bade him good night, then went back to their pipes. Longarm picked up his hat from the small table beside the front door where he had set it earlier. Silvia opened the door and stepped outside with him, pulling the door closed behind them. That surprised Longarm a little.

She strolled beside him down the short walk to the road, between the shapes of the cactus garden that had turned eerie in the emerging moonlight. Night had fallen with desert suddenness, leaving a sky of black velvet dotted with diamond stars overhead. Some of the day's heat lingered, but a cooling breeze had sprung up.

"It is a beautiful night," Silvia said quietly.

"That it is," agreed Longarm. He paused at the end of the walk. She stood close to him, and he looked down into her face. The silvery light of moon and stars shone on her smooth, rounded cheeks. Longarm wanted very much to kiss her, but she gave no indication that was why she had come out here with him.

Instead, she touched his arm again and said, "If you find out anything about Jack, you will tell me, no?"

"Of course I will," Longarm promised. Maybe not right

away, he added mentally, but once he discovered Jack Ralston's fate, he would make sure this young woman knew of it eventually.

"Thank you, Señor Ralston."

"Maybe you ought to call me Custis," Longarm suggested.

He saw her smile. "Custis," she repeated. "It is an unusual name."

"I've put up with it for a heap of years."

"It suits you somehow. You are an unusual man."

Did she want him to kiss her? She was standing mighty close, and her hand was on his arm, and Longarm could practically taste the sweet warmth of those full lips. . . .

"Good night, Custis," she said, then turned and walked toward the house. Longarm couldn't do a thing but think, *Damn it!* as he watched her go. If there had been a chance, he had just missed it.

Grinning wryly to himself, he turned and started walking along the road toward the main part of Presidio. As he came closer, he saw the lights of the saloons and heard the tinkly strains of piano music floating through the night air. The thought of a nightcap before he turned in suddenly appealed to him. He headed toward the trading post, knowing that the bar there stocked Maryland rye.

He was just passing one of the darkened buildings when he heard the fast shuffle of footsteps behind him on the dusty road. He swung around, his hand going instinctively toward his gun, but before he could reach it something exploded right in his face.

41

Chapter 9

Longarm stumbled backward, knocked off balance by the brutal, unexpected blow. Skyrockets sizzled through his brain as he tried to catch himself and keep from falling. He was only partially successful. He went to one knee as he saw several vague shapes rushing at him.

He had the presence of mind to know he couldn't allow his attackers to trap him on the ground. If they did, they could stomp him to death before he was able to get back up. He reached out, guided by the instincts he had developed during long, dangerous years as a lawman, and caught hold of the boot that was coming toward him in a vicious kick. He wrenched hard, and sent the man who went with the boot tumbling off his feet and into the path of the other attackers.

Longarm heard muffled curses as he forced himself back to his own feet. Hauling himself upright, he reached for his Colt again, only to find that the holster was empty. The gun must have slipped out when he nearly fell.

There wasn't time to look for it. A couple of the men were back up and coming toward him again. Longarm's head hurt like blazes, and his eyesight was a little blurry. He saw a fist coming at him, and managed to duck out of the way, but as he did another blow pounded into his side from the second man. He staggered.

42

This time he didn't go down even part of the way. He shot out his right fist in a straight punch that collided with somebody's jaw. The impact shivered back up his arm, and Longarm found the feeling quite satisfying. He set his feet and swung a left at the other man, but the hombre slipped it, blocking the punch with his forearm. He bored in, swinging short, vicious jabs at Longarm's body.

Longarm knew he couldn't stand up long under this kind of punishment. He lowered his head, hunched his shoulders, and threw himself forward with a roar of anger. His arms went around his nearest opponent and he left his feet. The flying tackle sent both men sprawling to the ground, but Longarm landed on top and landed hard. He heard the *whoof!* as all the air was driven out of the man's lungs. Longarm rolled to the side as the man lay there limp and gasping for breath.

Another kick missed him narrowly as he surged back to his feet, calling on all the finely honed strength in his body to do so. A dark shape came at him from the left side. Longarm threw an elbow into the man's throat and heard him gagging. At the same time, he pivoted to his left, making himself a smaller target for the third man. That man's lunge carried him into Longarm, who grabbed his shirt, stuck out a hip for leverage, and tossed the man neatly through the air. Longarm had learned the fancy move from his friend Ki, up on Jessie Starbuck's Circle Star ranch; he didn't use it often, but it came in handy every now and then.

Two of his attackers were down, and the third one was sort of stumbling around and holding his throat, trying not to strangle. That man reached for his hip as he gargled out obscenities, and Longarm knew what was coming next. He threw himself forward and down as the man's gun came up and geysered orange flame.

It wasn't a blind jump just to get out of the way of the flying lead, although Longarm was mighty glad to hear the slug whistle past well above his head. He had spotted something dark lying on the ground, and he reached for it now as he sprawled in the dust. His fingers closed

43

around the familiar walnut grips of his Colt.

Still lying flat, he tipped the barrel of the gun up and squeezed the trigger. The revolver bucked against his palm as he fired. The man looming a few feet away stumbled back. His gun slipped from his hand and thudded to the street.

He must not have been hit too badly, though, because he was able to whirl around and break into a run. Now that he was disarmed and Longarm wasn't, the hombre didn't have any interest in continuing this fight. Longarm pushed himself up onto his knees and tried to draw a bead on the fleeing man's legs. He didn't want to kill the son of a bitch, just stop him. It would have been a tricky shot anyway, given the bad light, and Longarm was still a little addled from that initial blow. He squeezed the trigger, but the running man never slowed down as he ducked around the corner of a building and disappeared.

Longarm bit back a curse and looked around hurriedly for the other two. They were gone as well, he saw. Must have regained their senses enough to crawl off into the shadows, he told himself.

It didn't really matter, he thought as he got shakily to his feet. He had a pretty good idea who had jumped him—Art Calhorn and the other two men he'd run off from the school that afternoon.

He was considering giving chase to the man he'd shot when somebody down the street yelled, "Hey!" Longarm thought the voice belonged to Sam Horne. He holstered his gun before turning around slowly. He had no idea how trigger-happy the Ranger was, and he didn't want to give Horne any excuse to start shooting.

Sure enough, Horne was trotting toward him, gun drawn. Longarm could see that much in the light that spilled through the windows of the buildings Horne passed. Several other people had emerged into the street, their attention drawn by the gunfire, but they were content to hang back and let Horne hurry along to see what had happened.

Horne drew to a stop a few yards away. He leveled the

pistol at Longarm and said, "Hold it right there, mister. Don't move."

"Wasn't planning to," said Longarm. "Take it easy, Ranger. It's me—Custis Ralston."

Horne snorted in disgust to show what he thought of Longarm's masquerade as the missing man's brother. Longarm didn't know who might be listening in the dark, though, and he wanted to maintain the pose if possible. He was grateful that Horne didn't give away the truth.

"What happened?" the Ranger asked. "I heard a couple of shots."

"Some fellas jumped me," Longarm replied. "Busted me across the face with something, then tried to stomp me into the ground. I wasn't of a mind to let 'em. So it was a pretty good fracas for a while, before one of them decided to turn it into a shooting scrap instead."

"Are you wounded?"

"Nope. The hombre who took a shot at me missed. I think I might've winged him, though." Longarm pointed. "He ran off around that building."

Horne finally holstered his gun as he came closer. "You got a match?" he asked. "Maybe we can find a blood trail." He seemed to have accepted Longarm's story, which came as a bit of a surprise to the big federal lawman. As hostile as Horne had been earlier in the day, Longarm had figured he would be more suspicious now.

Longarm dug out a lucifer and struck it, aware that he was making himself a target for anybody lurking out there in the dark with a Winchester, waiting to bushwhack him. He didn't think Calhorn would try it, though, not with a Texas Ranger standing right here beside him. He stepped over to the spot where the gunman had been, then bent over, looking for telltale drops of blood in the dust.

Horne grunted. "Don't see a thing but some scuffed-up footprints, and there's thousands of those on this street."

Longarm had to agree. He moved on, following the path the man had taken as he fled, and when the first match burned down, he lit another. The two lawmen reached the mouth of an alley without seeing any blood.

"Guess I didn't nick him after all," Longarm said as he shook out the second lucifer. "Bullet must've come close enough to spook him, though, since he dropped his own gun and took off for the tall and uncut."

"Could be right," agreed Horne. "Did you get a look at any of 'em?"

"Not so's you'd notice. I was a mite busy at the time. But I know who they were."

"Who?" Horne sounded surprised.

"Art Calhorn and two more of Gil Hoskins's riders. We had a run-in down at the school this afternoon. I had a feeling when they left that they'd be looking to settle the score with me."

"I heard about that," said Horne. "You make a habit of poking your nose in other people's business?"

"Seemed like the thing to do at the time," Longarm said coldly, "seeing as how they were making an old man dance by shooting at his feet."

"Benjamin Akin hasn't filed a complaint with me," said Horne.

"Would it do any good? I hear Hoskins is the big skookum he-wolf around here. In a lot of places, a man like that swings enough influence so that his riders get away with whatever they want."

"Not around here," Horne grated.

For some reason, Longarm believed him.

The Ranger angled his head toward his office. "Come on down the street with me," he said. "I'm glad you came along. Saves me the trouble of looking you up. I reckon we need to have another talk."

Longarm wasn't expecting that. He said, "You going to tell me to get out of town again?"

"Just come on," Horne snapped.

Longarm shrugged, nodded, and fell into step beside Horne. Maybe the Ranger was actually going to cooperate now.

But Longarm was going to believe that when he saw it.

Chapter 10

Horne let out a little whistle when he got a good look at Longarm's face in the light of the Ranger office. "Reckon you're goin' to have a pretty good pair of shiners by morning," he said. "What'd they do, slap you across the face with a two-by-four?"

"That's what it felt like," Longarm grumbled. Gingerly, he prodded at his nose with his fingertips. He decided it wasn't broken, even though it hurt like blazes.

"You ought to let our local sawbones take a look at you," suggested Horne. "No telling what getting hit in the head like that might do to a fella."

"I ain't addlepated," Longarm insisted. "This old noggin of mine is too hard for that. But I wouldn't mind sitting down for a spell and having a drink."

Horne waved at the broken-down old couch that sat against one wall of the office. "Have a seat. I can do something about that drink too." He went behind his desk and opened one of the drawers.

Longarm frowned suspiciously as he took off his hat, hung it on the rack just beside the door, and lowered himself on the couch, being careful to avoid the broken spring that poked through the cushions. What was going on here? he asked himself. Horne was almost being friendly now.

The Ranger took a couple of glasses and a bottle from

the desk. "This who-hit-John ain't fancy," he said, "but it's better'n the possum piss they serve in most of the saloons around here."

Longarm knew for a fact that he could've gotten a shot of Tom Moore over at the Fort Leaton trading post, but he didn't say anything while Horne was splashing whiskey into the glasses. He didn't want to do anything to spoil the Ranger's apparent good mood.

Maybe Horne thought that getting into a fight would make Longarm more likely to get out of Presidio and return to Denver. That was what Horne had wanted all along. If that was the case, though, the Ranger was going to be disappointed.

After being jumped like that, Longarm felt less like getting out of town than ever.

Horne handed Longarm one of the glasses and carried his own behind the desk, where he sat down in an old swivel chair and leaned back. He downed the whiskey, put the empty glass on the desk, and sighed.

Longarm took his time with his drink, figuring that as touchy as his head felt right now, too much of a jolt might not be good for it. He sipped the liquor, found it not too bad, and leaned back himself, cocking his right ankle on his left knee. He waited for Horne to start the ball rolling.

He didn't have to wait long. Horne said, "I've been thinking about it, and I reckon I don't have any choice but to cooperate with you, Marshal."

Longarm said, "We're after the same thing—getting those Army rifles back, or at least finding out who stole them and bringing the thieves to justice."

Horne grunted. "The Army doesn't *want* those rifles back."

Now that was something he hadn't known, Longarm thought with a frown. "Why the hell not?" he asked.

"Because they were gettin' rid of them in the first place. They're old Peabody conversions, and they're being replaced by trapdoor Springfields. The Army gathered up all they had at their forts in West Texas, and were sending them to Fort Bliss in El Paso to be shipped back east. I think they planned at one time on selling them to some of the state militias, but that deal fell through. I reckon they would've wound up being melted down for scrap metal."

"So the guns aren't any good?"

"Oh, they'll shoot, I suppose," Horne said. "Just not all that good. But still, in the wrong hands they could cause some mischief. That's why the government wants them found. They don't want Mexican revolutionaries shooting at President Diaz's troops with U.S. Army guns, whether they're obsolete or not."

Horne's mention of revolutionaries prompted Longarm to say, "Like Los Niños de Libertad?"

The Ranger leaned forward and frowned. "Where'd you hear about them?"

"Rumors back up the stage line. I'm told they don't really exist."

"Who told you that?"

Longarm shrugged. "Heard it around town." He didn't want Horne to get mad at Benjamin Akin.

"Well, they're real, all right," Horne said. "And it wouldn't surprise me a bit if they've got those rifles."

"You know who their leader is, or where they hole up?"

Horne shook his head. "You know what it's like over there across the border. Nobody talks, and people who want to disappear can vanish like grains of sand blown away by the wind."

That was true enough, thought Longarm. He took out a cheroot and said, "Tell me about the actual holdup."

"There was a convoy of three Army wagons with a handful of guards and outriders along with the drivers. Whoever held them up jumped the outriders first. Roped 'em and pulled them off their horses neat as you please, then knocked them out and tied them up. Then they hit the convoy as it went through a draw in the hills north of here. Shot the leaders on each of the mule teams to stop them. The guards didn't fight back when they saw they were surrounded. I guess they didn't figure some crates of old rifles were worth dyin' over."

"They saw the thieves?"

Horne shrugged. "If you can call it that. Everybody in the bunch was wrapped up in serapes and wore big sombreros. None of the soldier boys got a good look at them."

Longarm lit the cheroot and puffed on it for a moment as he thought. Then he said with a frown, "None of the soldiers were killed?"

"Well . . . no. Come to think of it, they weren't. There weren't many shots fired, and nobody got hurt except those mules." Horne clasped his hands together on the desk. "But there could be a reason for that. Those revolutionaries didn't want the U.S. Army coming after them. They have enough trouble with the Mexican Army."

"You're convinced it was rebels who took the guns, not a band of outlaws like Mendoza's bunch?"

"You *are* well informed, aren't you? You hear about Mendoza in the same place you heard about Los Niños?"

"That's right."

Horne shook his head. "It wasn't Mendoza. If it had been, every one of those troopers would have died slow and painful-like."

Longarm tended to agree with that opinion. Now that he knew more about the actual theft of the rifles, he felt certain that the revolutionaries were to blame for it. And there was still the matter of Jack Ralston's disappearance.

"What about Ralston?" he asked. "How long has he been missing?"

"Several weeks," Horne replied with a scowl. "Nearly a month, in fact."

"When were the rifles stolen?"

"Going on six weeks ago. Jack showed up a couple of days after the Army notified me of the robbery. He was able to get here so fast because he was already in Ozona wrapping up a rustling case when he got word to come over here and investigate. We agreed from the first that he'd work undercover, and he came up with the idea of posing as a prospector. That'd give him an excuse for nosing around the mountains on the other side of the border."

"He spent enough time in town to get friendly with some of the locals, though," Longarm pointed out.

"You're talking about Silvia Gonzalez and her brother?" Horne shrugged. "Jack was a good-looking young fella. It was natural that him and the Gonzalez girl would take an interest in one another. But he was looking for leads to the rifles at the same time. Lots of kids from across the border come to that school, and they have relatives in other villages. Jack tried to find out if Silvia had heard about anything odd goin' on."

"He could've tipped his hand without meaning to," suggested Longarm. "Silvia Gonzalez strikes me as pretty smart."

Horne nodded. "Yeah, but I can't see her doing anything to Ralston, even if she suspected what he was up to. She liked him too much for that."

"I never thought she plugged him," Longarm said dryly. "I just figured she might not tell him what he wanted to know."

"Maybe not. Jack and I didn't have that much contact. He couldn't risk his cover by hangin' around the Ranger post all the time. Anyway, the last I saw of him, he was planning on going across the river again. He'd been over a couple of times but hadn't been able to come up with anything."

"And this time he never came back," said Longarm.

"This time he never came back," agreed Horne.

Both lawmen were silent for a moment. Finally, Longarm said, "If Ralston found Los Niños, would they have killed him? They didn't kill anybody when they stole the rifles, if that was really them."

"I honestly don't know. But if he ran into Mendoza instead . . ." Horne shook his head. "Mendoza would torture and murder just about any gringo he came across, lawman or not. Ralston wouldn't have had much of a chance against that bunch."

Longarm figured that was probably what had happened to the missing Ranger. He nodded slowly and then stood up. He was starting to feel drowsy. "Thanks for the drink and the information. Reckon I'll go over to the hotel and try to get some sleep."

"What are you going to do about the investigation?"

"Pretending to be Ralston's brother seems to be working, and it gives me an excuse to poke around too. I'll keep it up for a while."

"Be careful," growled Horne. "I got one missing man to worry about already. I don't need another one."

"Why, Ranger Horne, you *do* care," Longarm said with a grin.

"You won't be laughing in the morning," Horne predicted, "when you see what your face looks like."

Chapter 11

Longarm got his gear from the stage station and went over to the hotel, registering as Custis Ralston. The clerk looked at his face said nothing, handing him the room key.

Before going to sleep, Longarm thought quite a bit about what he had learned about the case from Sam Horne. For one thing, he didn't see what was so damned urgent about it that he'd had to be rousted out of Julie Cassidy's arms in the middle of the night. The rifles had been stolen almost six weeks earlier, and Jack Ralston had been missing for nearly a month. But that was typical of how things worked in Washington, he reminded himself. A problem could sit there and hang fire for a long time. Then suddenly, for no apparent reason, something had to be done about it *now*.

After staring at the ceiling for a while as he turned the information over in his mind, Longarm finally rolled onto his side and went to sleep. He dreamed about goats, of all things, and how he was chasing a bunch of the critters around and around a corral. He never could catch them, and the men who were sitting around on the top rail of the corral, watching, just laughed and laughed at him. Especially Art Calhorn, who slapped his leg and whooped with hilarity every time Longarm lunged at one of the goats and missed.

He woke up in the morning still tired, headachy, and mad as hell.

The same clerk was on duty at the desk in the lobby. He looked up at Longarm as he came downstairs, and this time the man's eyes widened in surprise. Longarm already knew what the clerk was looking at; he had seen the same sight in the mirror over the basin as he shaved. Both eyes had black rings around them, and the bruises extended to his nose and the sides of his face. He looked like a damned raccoon.

"I . . . I'm sorry, Mr. Ralston," the clerk began, but Longarm waved off the apology.

"Don't worry about it, old son. I know I look like a mule kicked me. What I want you to tell me is where to find the nearest stable where I can rent a horse."

The clerk put his hands flat on the desk and leaned forward to say in a conspiratorial tone, "I heard that you were looking for your missing brother. I wish you luck in your search, Mr. Ralston. I hope you find him."

"Thanks," said Longarm. He was glad the word was getting around town that he was Jack Ralston's brother and that he was searching for the missing man. That might help. "Now, about that stable . . ."

"Of course. You just go right down the street to Newcomb's livery."

The clerk gave Longarm directions to the stable. Before going down there, Longarm stopped in the hotel dining room and got a quick breakfast of ham, eggs, flapjacks, and several cups of coffee. The meal helped his headache, and he felt almost human again as he walked to the livery stable.

It was early, but the trading post down the street was already doing a brisk business. Longarm passed the Ranger post on the opposite side of the street, and saw Sam Horne standing in the doorway of the adobe building, one shoulder leaned against the jamb. The Ranger gave Longarm a pleasant nod.

Longarm still wasn't sure what had motivated Horne's change in attitude, but he was reminded of the old proverb about the gift horse. Right now, he was just glad that Horne had decided not to continue giving him grief. It wasn't as if Longarm had *asked* to come down here and take over the investigation. He was just following orders.

Newcomb was also the town blacksmith as well as owner of the livery stable. He was a tall, burly man with a wild shock of black hair and a long, tangled black beard that made him look a little like an Old Testament prophet, Longarm thought. He pumped Longarm's hand with a grip like iron and said, "Mighty pleased to meet you, Mr. Ralston. I sure hope you find that brother of yours. Jack was a mighty nice fella."

Jack Ralston had surely made an impression on the citizens of Presidio in the short time he had been there. Longarm nodded and said, "I'm going to do my best, Mr. Newcomb, but right now I need to rent a horse from you and maybe get some directions."

"The horse we can manage," Newcomb replied. "Got a sorrel that's a good saddle mount. Where do you need to go?"

"Out to Gil Hoskins's ranch."

Newcomb frowned. "I can tell you how to get there, but why would you want to go that way? Jack disappeared on the other side of the border."

"This is something else I have to take care of before I go looking for my brother," Longarm explained. "Just some personal business."

"All right. You need tack too?"

"Just a harness and bridle. I've got my own saddle over at the hotel."

Longarm paid for the rental of the sorrel and led the animal back over to the hotel after Newcomb had told him how to find Gil Hoskins's Leaning H Ranch. It was northeast of town, where a little creek that flowed into the Rio Grande watered a valley between the Santiago Mountains and the Tierra Vieja range. Longarm figured he would be able to reach the ranch headquarters in a couple of hours of riding.

That estimate was off, but not by much. It was not long after mid-morning when Longarm, following a well-worn trail from Presidio, came within sight of the Leaning H. The house was built on the banks of the creek. A few small cottonwoods and mesquite trees grew around it. The house was stone, the barns adobe. The place looked old, as if it had been there a long time before Gil Hoskins took it over. That was entirely possible, thought Longarm. It had probably belonged originally to some Mexican *hacendado,* in the days when Texas was still part of Mexico.

He had been seeing Leaning H cattle for quite a while, so he wasn't surprised when he reached the ranch headquarters. As he rode in, several dogs raced out to greet him, barking loudly and racing around the hooves of the sorrel. The commotion brought a couple of men from the nearest barn, and Hoskins himself stepped out onto the porch of the ranch house.

The rancher saw Longarm, recognized him as a fellow passenger from the stagecoach, and raised a hand in greeting. During the ride out there, Longarm had thought back over the journey, retracing every mile in his mind, and he was fairly certain he had never told Hoskins his name. He hadn't learned the rancher's name until he arrived in Presidio and described him to Silvia and Akin.

"Hello," Hoskins called in a friendly tone. "I didn't expect to see you again. Light and come inside out of the heat. What the devil happened to your face?"

Longarm nodded his thanks. He glanced toward the two men who had come from the barn. One of them, he saw, was Art Calhorn. The other was a stranger, but he looked just as rough as the two men who had been with Calhorn at the school the day before.

"Obliged," Longarm said as he swung down from the saddle and looped the sorrel's reins over the hitch rack in front of the house. He stepped up into the shade of the porch and offered Hoskins his hand. "Had a little accident last night. That's the reason my face looks like this. Name's Custis Ralston."

"Not Jack Ralston's brother?" Hoskins asked as he shook hands.

Had Ralston made friends with *everybody* in the county before vanishing?

Longarm said, "That's right."

"Well, hell, you should've introduced yourself while we were on the stage. I knew your brother."

Longarm had already noticed that most folks spoke of knowing Jack Ralston in the past tense. They probably figured the same thing he did, that Ralston was dead. A man didn't just disappear south of the border like that without something bad happening to him.

"Have you come to Texas to look for him?" Hoskins went on.

Longarm nodded. "Yeah, but that's not why I rode out here today. I'd like to talk to your foreman."

Hoskins gestured toward Calhorn and the other man and said, "He's right over there. Come here a minute, Art."

Calhorn looked reluctant, but he walked over to the porch, trailed by the other cowboy. Longarm noticed that Calhorn had some scrapes on his face, and when he said, "What is it, Boss?" his voice came out in a harsh gargle. Longarm knew then that Calhorn was the man he had elbowed in the throat. Calhorn went on angrily, "Whatever this fella's been tellin' you is a pack of lies."

Hoskins looked surprised. "You two know each other?"

"We've met," Longarm said dryly. "At the school in town yesterday, and then last night when Calhorn and a couple of his pards jumped me."

"That's a damned lie, I tell you!" Calhorn blazed.

Hoskins had been friendlier here on his ranch than he had been on the stagecoach, but his air of affability dropped away now that Longarm had accused one of his men of something. "What's this all about?" he demanded. "I want you to know right now, Ralston, that I won't stand for anybody trying to frame my men."

57

"What happened between Calhorn and me ain't nobody else's business," Longarm said coolly. "I stomp my own snakes, so I'm not looking for you to take a hand in that, Hoskins. Besides, even with odds of three to one, Calhorn and his pards are the ones who took a licking."

Calhorn just glared at him silently.

Longarm slipped a cheroot out of his shirt pocket and went on. "What I'm here to see Calhorn about is the rustling."

"Rustling?" Calhorn and Hoskins yelped at the same time.

Longarm lit the cheroot with a lucifer, then with the cigar clenched between his teeth, asked, "What did you do with those goats you stole, Calhorn?"

Chapter 12

Calhorn's upper lip curled in a snarl and his hand started toward the butt of the gun on his hip. "You bastard! I oughta—"

"Art!" Hoskins's voice ripped out, stopping his foreman's move. "No gunplay."

"But, Boss," Calhorn practically pleaded, "you heard what this sorry son of a bitch said."

Hoskins turned his attention to Longarm. "I heard," he said grimly. "What's this all about, Ralston? I told you, I won't stand for one of my men being framed."

Longarm took the cheroot from his lips and blew out a cloud of smoke. "Nobody's trying to frame anybody. I don't even care whether or not Calhorn gets thrown in the hoosegow for goat rustling. I just want those goats back where they belong, at the school in Presidio."

Calhorn stared at Longarm and declared, "He's crazy!"

Longarm shook his head. "Nope. I should've seen it right off, but I reckon what with worrying about my brother being missing and all, I wasn't paying that much attention to anything else. Calhorn's got a grudge against Señorita Gonzalez and the school, so I figure he's the most likely one to have run off their goats." A faint smile tugged at the corners of his mouth. "I reckon you could say it came to me in a dream."

"Sounds to me like you're either drunk or feeble-minded," Calhorn said sneeringly. "I never stole any goats."

"Rustling any sort of livestock is a serious charge, Ralston," Gil Hoskins said solemnly. "Do you have any proof of your accusations?"

"Well, no," Longarm admitted. "But I thought maybe you'd let me take a look around your ranch so I can see if I can find those goats." He glanced at Calhorn. "If they ain't already *cabrito,* that is."

"We have a small herd of goats of our own," Hoskins said. "You're welcome to take a look at them." The rancher glanced at his foreman. "That all right with you, Art?"

Calhorn was still sneering. "Sure, Boss. I reckon it's best to humor a crazy man."

As soon as Calhorn said that, Longarm knew he wouldn't find the school's goats among the Leaning H herd. He wasn't sure how he would have picked them out anyway, since one goat looked pretty much like another. He had counted on the accusation making Calhorn lose his temper and give something away, but so far Calhorn was maintaining his composure. Longarm decided he'd have to prod him a little more.

"Maybe what I should do is bring Silvia Gonzalez out here so she could take a look at the goats," he said. "She'd be more likely to recognize them than I would, and then she could tell you herself how she feels about you, Calhorn."

Calhorn's face flushed a darker red. "What do you mean by that?"

Hoskins put in, "And what was that you said earlier about Art having a grudge against the Gonzalez girl and the school?"

Longarm turned back to the rancher and held up one finger on his left hand. "Calhorn's sweet on the girl, but she won't give him the time of day. That's the grudge against her." He lifted another finger. "And all of your riders know how you feel about educating those Mexican

60

children, Hoskins. That's the second grudge."

It was Hoskins's turn to flush with anger. "What do you mean by that?" he demanded. "I don't have anything against that school. I just don't think that old fool Akin should be filling their heads with nonsense. He's just trying to stir up trouble."

Longarm shrugged, figuring that Hoskins had just proved his point for him. It was time to switch back to Calhorn. "I'm not completely satisfied that Calhorn here didn't have something to do with my brother's disappearance."

"What!" exclaimed Calhorn. Again his hand started toward his gun. "You son of a—"

Longarm waited a beat to see if Hoskins was going to stop Calhorn this time. After a second, though, he couldn't afford to wait any longer. His hand went across his body and palmed out the Colt in the time it took Calhorn to wrap his fingers around the butt of his own gun.

"I wouldn't, old son," Longarm said quietly as he pointed the Colt at Calhorn.

Calhorn froze. The tension on the porch was thick now. If Calhorn finished his draw, Longarm could down him easily before he got off a shot. But that left Hoskins and the other ranch hand, both of whom were armed and would have Longarm in a cross fire if they opened up. At least one of them would probably be able to get a slug into him before he could stop them.

"Damn it, you'd better explain yourself," snapped Hoskins to Longarm. "And make it quick."

Longarm's gun didn't budge. Neither did Calhorn, who stood there gripping his gun but not drawing it—yet. Longarm said, "Like I told you, Calhorn's sweet on Silvia Gonzalez. But Silvia was interested in my brother. Could be Calhorn decided to get rid of him so he'd have a clear field with Silvia."

"Now that *is* a lie," rasped Calhorn. "I might've taken those blasted goats, but I didn't kill anybody. I wouldn't even let the cook make stew out of those damned animals!"

Well, he'd finally prodded Calhorn into one admission of guilt anyway, thought Longarm. While it was possible that Calhorn could have had something to do with Ralston's disappearance, Longarm considered the idea pretty far-fetched. He'd been convinced of the foreman's guilt in the goat rustling, though.

"You took those goats, Art?" Hoskins said harshly.

Calhorn was trembling a little with rage as he stared at Longarm. "Yeah, and I'd do it again!"

"What about Jack Ralston?"

"I didn't like him, but I didn't do anything to him, Boss. I swear it."

Longarm believed Calhorn, and evidently so did Hoskins. "There you are, Ralston," the rancher said. "You've got the answers you wanted. Now put that gun away."

Slowly, Longarm lowered the Colt and holstered it, but he was ready to draw again if need be.

"I'll see that the goats are returned to the school," Hoskins went on, "with my apologies for what happened. Art, I won't abide a thief on the Leaning H. Draw your pay and get out."

Calhorn's eyes widened in shock. "But, Boss—"

"Now," said Hoskins.

"Damn it, you don't like that school or those Mexican kids any more than I do," Calhorn said. "You two-faced bastard."

For a second, Longarm thought Hoskins was going to step down off the porch and slap Calhorn. The rancher controlled himself with a visible effort and said again, "Get out, Art. Get off my land."

"I won't forget this," Calhorn said. Glaring at Longarm and Hoskins, he turned and stalked toward the bunkhouse. The other man went with him. Longarm kept an eye on Calhorn, just in case he tried to turn around quickly and go for his gun.

"I'm sorry, Ralston," Hoskins said. Wearily, the man rubbed a hand over his weathered face. "It's true I don't like that Yankee schoolteacher, but I never intended for any of my men to cause trouble for him."

"They've been trying to drive Akin out of Presidio for a while," Longarm said. "You can ask Sam Horne about it if you don't believe me."

"I believe you," Hoskins said grimly. "But I'll ask you to believe me when I say that Art Calhorn didn't have anything to do with the disappearance of your brother. Art's not a killer."

Longarm didn't say anything. He had his own opinion about Art Calhorn.

"For another thing, your brother vanished below the border," Hoskins went on. "People saw him ride across the river, and he never came back. Art hasn't been off the ranch long enough to have followed him across the border and done anything to him."

"You're sure of that?"

"I'm certain," Hoskins said. "I work the range with my men. I know where they are."

"You were just up in Santa Fe on business," Longarm pointed out. "We rode down together on the train."

"But a month ago, when Jack Ralston vanished, I was here on the Leaning H every day, and so was Calhorn."

Longarm considered this for a second, then nodded. "That's good enough for me," he said.

Calhorn came out of the bunkhouse with a war bag slung over his shoulder. The other man had saddled Calhorn's horse while the ex-foreman was inside. Calhorn took the reins and led the mount over to the house. "I'll have the wages I got comin' to me," he said to Hoskins.

"I'll get them," the rancher said. "You wait here." Hoskins turned to Longarm and said, "You'd better head back to town, Ralston. I'll have those goats brought back to the school later today. You have my word on it."

Longarm nodded. "Thanks." He knew what Hoskins was doing. Hoskins wanted him well on the way back to Presidio before Calhorn left the ranch. That way there wouldn't be any chance of trouble between them. Longarm was willing to go along with that. All he'd really wanted was to get the school's goats back and find out if

63

Calhorn had an alibi in Jack Ralston's disappearance, and he had accomplished both of those things.

He untied the sorrel's reins and swung up into the saddle. Before he turned to ride away, he met Art Calhorn's eyes for a moment. Calhorn's gaze was full of hatred. Calhorn was already an enemy, but now he was a worse one, with a bigger score to settle.

If they ever crossed paths again, thought Longarm, the air would probably smell of gun smoke.

Chapter 13

Silvia Gonzalez threw her arms around Longarm's neck and impulsively hugged him. "*Gracias,* Señor Ralston!" she said. "Benjamin and I cannot thank you enough."

The way she was pressed up against him so tightly was a pretty nice expression of gratitude, thought Longarm. If she kept rubbing her pelvis against his groin that way, she was going to feel hard evidence of just how nice it was.

She stepped back, though, before Longarm's shaft could grow erect enough to start prodding her in the belly. Smiling up at him, she said, "We should have known that Art Calhorn had something to do with the loss of our goats. He has been causing trouble for us for a long time. I never really understood why he disliked us so."

Longarm didn't want to tell her that she had gotten Calhorn so hot and bothered that he'd been unable to think straight when she brushed him off. Calhorn had wanted to pay her back for that unintended slight, and if he could curry favor with his boss at the same time, so much the better.

"Some of Hoskins's men brought back the goats?" he asked.

Silvia nodded, and Benjamin Akin said, "Yes, they rode in with the goats this afternoon. The children were over-joyed. Those goats are almost like pets to them."

Longarm, Silvia, and Akin were standing in the school. Classes were over for the day. Longarm could hear the goats blatting in the pen behind the building. It was a sound that reminded him of his childhood on the farm in West Virginia. They'd always had goats around.

"You will join us for supper again?" Silvia asked. "It is the least I can do to repay you."

Longarm grinned. "I'd be much obliged. The food in the hotel dining room ain't bad, but it ain't like a home-cooked meal either."

Silvia came up on her toes and brushed a kiss across Longarm's cheek. "Thank you again, Custis," she said in a half whisper.

Longarm agreed to come to the Gonzalez house a little before dusk for supper, then left the school and walked over to the trading post at Fort Leaton. He went into the saloon and saw that the burly Stanley Gonzalez was once again on duty behind the bar.

Stanley grinned at him and greeted him by saying, "Ah, the finder of lost goats!"

Longarm's eyebrows quirked. "Has that story already gotten around?"

"But of course," said Stanley. "Presidio is a small town. And Art Calhorn has already been in." Stanley's face grew more serious. "He was drinking in a cantina owned by one of my cousins. Drinking a great deal, as an angry man will. It is said he swore vengeance on you, Señor Ralston."

Longarm shrugged. "I've had fellas hold a grudge against me before. It ain't anything new."

"Calhorn, though, he is a bad one," Stanley said with a shake of his head. "You must watch your back."

"I always do," Longarm assured him.

The bartender's mood brightened. "You are coming to supper at our house again tonight?"

"Your sister already invited me."

"I thought she probably would. You are most welcome in our *casa*."

Longarm picked up the mug of beer that Stanley placed on the bar in front of him and sipped from it. "Now that

that goat business is out of the way, I've got to start think-ing about finding my brother."

Stanley frowned. "You would go across the border to look for him?"

"That's where he disappeared," Longarm said with a shrug. "I don't know where else to start."

"If there is any way Silvia and I can help you . . ."

"Keep your eyes and ears open," Longarm said. "If you hear anything about my brother, be it rumors or whatever, please let me know."

Stanley's head bobbed up and down. "This we will do," he pledged.

After finishing the beer, Longarm went back to the hotel to shave and change his shirt before he went to the Gonza-lez house for supper. When he came out of the hotel, he saw Sam Horne lounging in one of the chairs on the porch. The Ranger looked up at him and said, "I hear tell you got Art Calhorn fired from the Leaning H for goat rustling."

Longarm shrugged. "When you say it that way, it sounds a mite humorous. Calhorn didn't think it was very funny, though."

"He wouldn't," Horne said. "He's the sort to hold a grudge. Reckon you already know that, though, after what happened last night."

Everybody seemed to be concerned for his welfare, Long-arm thought. It was downright touching. He said, "I'm not worried about Calhorn. I've got bigger fish to fry."

Horne dropped his voice so that only Longarm could hear him. "Ralston," he said, and Longarm knew he was referring to the missing Ranger, not to the false identity Longarm had adopted.

"That's right," Longarm nodded. "I hope to get a line on him soon."

Horne got to his feet. "Keep me advised," he said, still quietly. Longarm nodded again, and the Ranger turned to step down off the porch and start back toward his office.

Longarm walked toward the river, then turned along it on the path that led to the Gonzalez house. He was about to knock on the door when it was opened and Stanley

67

stood back with a sweeping gesture. "Come in," Stanley said with a smile.

Longarm frowned a little. Stanley must have been watching for him, and now this effusive welcome made him feel a mite suspicious. He stepped into the house, and a dozen or more voices suddenly burst into song.

A grin stretched across Longarm's face when he saw the group of children standing there singing a happy Mexican song. Most of them were dressed in rather ragged clothes, but their faces were scrubbed clean and they were smiling. Silvia Gonzalez and Benjamin Akin stood with them, one of the adults at each end of the double row of children. The littlest ones were up front, but most of the ones in back were more than half grown. Some of the boys, in fact, were taller than Silvia and Akin. Longarm knew without asking that he was looking at the students from the school.

When they finished the song, Longarm applauded and told them, "That was mighty nice. I ain't been serenaded in quite a spell."

Silvia stepped toward him. "The children wanted to thank you for rescuing our goats and seeing that they were returned to us. They call you the Savior of Goats."

"I've been called a lot of things," Longarm admitted, "but never that, leastways not that I can recollect." He nodded to the children. *"Muchas gracias."*

"De nada, señor," said the oldest of the boys with a solemn expression on his face. He stepped forward and shook hands with Longarm, and the others followed suit, filing past him to say their thanks individually.

When the children had left, Benjamin Akin said, "I believe the students have a new hero to go along with the patriots of the Revolution we are studying."

Longarm shook his head. "I appreciate the sentiment, but I ain't no hero, Mr. Akin. Just a fella trying to do what good he can."

"And what do you think the definition of a hero *is,* Mr. Ralston, eh?"

Longarm chuckled. "I learned a long time ago never to argue with schoolteachers, sir."

68

Silvia was bringing food from the kitchen. "Come, sit down," she told them. "Supper is ready."

The meal was every bit as good as the one the night before. Longarm enjoyed the food and the glass of brandy he shared afterward with Stanley and Akin. The men were smoking when Silvia rejoined them.

"Now that you have come to our aid, I suppose you will be resuming your search for your brother?" she said to Longarm as she sat down.

"I reckon so. I never intended to get mixed up in this business with the goats, but once it came to me that it must've been Calhorn who took them, I knew I couldn't let it go until I'd done something about it."

Silvia nodded. "But a man's brother, he is much more important than some goats."

Longarm inclined his head toward her. "I really need to find Jack," he said.

Silvia looked at Stanley, who returned her gaze impassively. His expression gave away nothing. Benjamin Akin, however, was frowning, and his lips drew together as they did whenever he disapproved of something. He didn't like what Silvia was about to say.

She said it anyway. "We can help you, Custis. We have heard that a strange gringo has been seen recently in a village on the other side of the border."

Longarm sat up straighter, not bothering to try to conceal his interest since Ralston's real brother certainly wouldn't have. "You think it was Jack?" he asked. Was it possible that the missing Texas Ranger could still be alive after all?

"It could have been," said Silvia. "It was said this man had yellow hair, like your brother."

"Was he in Ojinaga?"

Silvia shook her head. "No, the report came from a much smaller village, San Ramone. It is miles away in the foothills of the mountains."

"But you can tell me how to get there, can't you?" asked Longarm.

"I can do better than that," Silvia said with a smile. "I will take you there myself."

Chapter 14

"I don't think that's a good idea," Benjamin Akin said
before Longarm could make any reply to Silvia's suggestion.

"Nor do I," added Stanley. "It is dangerous below the
border, as you well know, Silvia."

She tossed her long black hair back defiantly. "I do not
mind running the risk if it will help Señor Ralston find
Jack. He has been a good friend to us, as his brother was
before him."

Akin and Stanley both turned toward Longarm. "Surely
you will not allow Silvia to place herself in danger this
way, Mr. Ralston," said Akin.

It was about time they got around to asking him,
thought Longarm. Not that he disagreed with the senti-
ments they were expressing. He said to Silvia, "I think it
would be better if you'd just tell me how to get to San
Ramone and then you stay here in Presidio."

Her expression was still defiant as she said, "What if I
refuse?"

"Then I'd be mighty sorry, and I'd find somebody else
to tell me how to get to San Ramone."

Stanley said, "That I can do, *señor*. You take the main
trail south from Ojinaga for five miles—"

"Oh!" Silvia exclaimed. "I am the one who brings Señor Ralston the news of his brother being seen, and you conspire against me!"

"The gringo who was spotted in San Ramone might not have been Jack," Longarm pointed out. "And your brother and Mr. Akin just want you to be safe. For that matter, so do I."

Silvia glared around at the three of them, then threw up her hands. "There is nothing I can do!" she said, and with a rustle of skirts, she marched indignantly out of the room.

"I am sorry, Señor Ralston," Stanley said. "It was not our intention to anger Silvia. She has a temper that is sometimes *muy caliente*."

Longarm had thought Silvia looked lovelier than ever with her eyes flashing fire that way, but he couldn't very well say that to her brother and her mentor. Instead he told them, "I appreciate her wanting to help, but I reckon it'd be better if I went to San Ramone alone."

"I would take you myself, *señor,* but I must tend the bar at the trading post."

Longarm nodded. "I understand. Just tell me how to get there, and that'll be fine."

"As I said, you take the main trail south from Ojinaga for five miles. . . ."

Longarm listened attentively to the directions and filed them away in his brain. He was a professional, and this was part of his job.

But a part of his mind was still thinking about how pretty Silvia Gonzalez was when she was mad.

Longarm was up early the next morning. Dressed in jeans and a butternut shirt, he carried his saddle and Winchester down to Newcomb's livery and made arrangements to rent the same sorrel again.

"Don't know how long I'll be gone," he told the burly liveryman. "I'll take good care of the horse, though."

"Got a lead on your brother's whereabouts?" asked Newcomb.

"Maybe," Longarm said. He didn't go into detail.

"You best be careful," Newcomb advised as he brought out the sorrel. "Things have been pretty quiet hereabouts during the past month or so, but that could change anytime."

Longarm nodded his thanks, saddled the horse, and led it down the street toward the Ranger post. Sam Horne stepped out to meet him, having seen him coming.

"Where are you going?" asked the Ranger.

"Place called San Ramone. I've heard that a stranger who matches the description of my brother was seen there recently."

Horne frowned, and Longarm halfway expected him to make some comment about Longarm starting to believe his own cover story. Instead, Horne said, "San Ramone's a pretty isolated place. No law there unless a troop of *rurales* happens to be close by, and that ain't likely most of the time. If you get into any trouble, you'll be on your own."

Longarm nodded. "That's what I'm used to."

"Well, be careful." Horne sighed. "I expect in another six weeks or so, I'll be explaining to whoever comes looking for you how *you* disappeared."

Longarm chuckled and said, "Thanks for the confidence."

He led the sorrel over to Fort Leaton and tied it outside the trading post. The bar was open, since it never really closed, but it was too early in the day for Stanley Gonzalez to be working behind the hardwood. Instead, a bald man with a prominent Adam's apple stood there, aimlessly polishing the bar with a rag. Longarm didn't go in. He turned the other way and entered the trading post itself.

When he emerged ten minutes later, the pair of saddlebags slung over his shoulder were filled with enough supplies to last him several days. He had a couple of full canteens as well. There were quite a few streams in the mountains on the other side of the border, but there was a lot of desert country too. A man never knew where a trail might take him.

He hung the saddlebags and tied them down, then grasped the reins and swung up into the saddle. As he turned the sorrel's head toward the Rio Grande, he thought about riding by the school to say good-bye to Silvia and Akin. He decided against it. Silvia had never returned to the main room of the Gonzalez house the night before, and Longarm didn't want to run the risk that she was still pouting this morning. He would see her when he returned to Presidio, he told himself. And maybe when he came back he would bring Jack Ralston with him, which would pretty much take care of any romantic chances he might have with Silvia, but that would be all right. There was no law saying that every gal he took a shine to had to wind up liking him too.

The sorrel's hooves clattered on the planks of the bridge connecting Presidio and Ojinaga. The settlement on the Mexican side of the river was smaller than the one on the American side, so it didn't take him long to ride through it, following a broad, dusty street that turned into the main trail leading south. Longarm urged the sorrel into a ground-eating trot. He wanted to make as much of the journey to San Ramone as possible before the day got too hot. Judging by the directions he had gotten from Stanley Gonzalez, he estimated he could reach the village by a little after noon.

The low, rugged peaks of the Sierra Grande range loomed in the distance to the southwest. San Ramone was in the foothills of those mountains. Between the river and the Sierra Grande was a strip of semi-arid landscape painted mostly in hues of brown and gray, with an occasional flash of green from the vegetation along a narrow creek. There was enough water to be found in these parts to allow a little farming, but it got more and more hardscrabble the farther one traveled from the Rio Grande and the Rio Conchos.

After less than an hour's ride, Longarm came to a cross-trail that ran generally east and west. He turned west. This route would take him directly toward the Sierra Grande and San Ramone. The sun rose higher behind him, and he could feel beads of sweat break out on the back of his neck and trickle down between his shoulder blades.

He felt something else too, a prickling that he mistook at first for the sting of the bright sunshine. He realized after a short time that it was caused by something else entirely.

It was his lawman's instinct, warning him that someone was following him.

Longarm reined in, lifted one of the canteens, and hipped around in the saddle to take a leisurely drink. To anyone watching him, it wouldn't be immediately apparent that what he was actually doing was checking his back trail. He didn't see anything, but as he screwed the cap back on the canteen, he felt confident that someone was behind him. He had lived this long by trusting his gut.

Art Calhorn was the first possibility that sprang to mind. Calhorn could have trailed him into Mexico with the idea of settling the score by gunning down Longarm where American law couldn't touch him. It was also possible that someone connected with the disappearance of Jack Ralston, identity as yet unknown, had followed him. After all, Longarm had hardly made a secret of his intention to go across the border to search for his "brother." He had thought all along that by being so open about his goal, he might be able to lure Ralston's killer or killers out of hiding. Of course, that was assuming that Ralston really was dead. . . .

He could go around and around in his head with this, Longarm thought, or he could just find out who was trailing him. He reached a small creek with a few cottonwoods and mesquite trees along its banks, and slipped out of the saddle. A slap on the sorrel's rump kept it trotting on across the stream and up the opposite bank. Longarm ducked into a clump of mesquite and crouched down. The sorrel wouldn't go far without a rider before it stopped to graze on one of the rare clumps of grass. It would probably ramble on far enough to fool whoever was following Longarm, though.

Sure enough, he had been crouched in the brush only

a few minutes when he heard the rapid hoofbeats of a horse. Whoever it was had stopped and hidden when Longarm paused earlier to take a drink, and now he was trying to make up for that delay. Longarm slipped his Colt out of its holster and waited until he heard the horse come down the gentle bank and splash into the water. Then he stepped out of the brush, leveled the revolver, and called out sharply, "Hold it right there, old son!"

On the horse in the middle of the creek, the rider cried out in surprise and twisted around in the saddle. Longarm saw the gun in the rider's hand coming up, and he almost squeezed the trigger of his Colt before he recognized the startled face of Silvia Gonzalez underneath the broad brim of a sombrero. He kept from shooting at the last split-instant of time.

Then the revolver in Silvia's hand boomed and geysered smoke and flame, and a giant iron fist smashed into Longarm's head, driving him back and down into some of the deepest darkness he had ever known.

Chapter 15

"Please don't die, Custis! Please do not die!"

At first, Longarm heard the desperately beseeching voice as if it were a faint whisper borne on the wind from a thousand miles away. Then, gradually, it became louder and clearer, and finally he recognized it as belonging to Silvia Gonzalez. He became aware too that he was lying on something warm and soft, and other than the fact that his head hurt like blazes, his current situation wasn't really all that bad. A sweet fragrance like flowers filled his nostrils, and then something tickled against his nose and made him turn his head to the side and sneeze.

That set off an explosion like a whole barrel of blasting powder going off inside his skull. He groaned.

"Custis!" Silvia exclaimed. "You are alive!"

He forced his eyes open, blinking several times as the light poked at them like daggers. When his vision finally cleared, he realized he was looking up at Silvia's worried face, as well as the undersides of her outthrust breasts in a white shirt. Her long, thick black hair hung down loosely, and it must have been a strand of it that had tickled his nose. From this vantage point, Longarm eventually figured out that he was lying on the ground with his head in Silvia's lap. The cottonwood branches that formed a backdrop for her lovely features told him they were on the bank of the creek.

"Do not move," she told him.

Longarm didn't intend to. For one thing, he figured that movement would set off more of those explosions in his head. For another, he liked the way his head was pillowed on the warmth of Silvia's thighs.

For a moment he couldn't remember what had happened and had no idea how he had come to be here like this. Slowly, memories began to filter back into his brain. He recalled how he had lain in wait in the brush beside the creek for whoever had been following him. Recalled as well how he had stepped out to challenge the rider, only to have her turn around and bring up a pistol and . . .

Shoot him. He remembered now. Silvia had shot him.

But judging by the worried look on her face and the way she was taking care of him, she hadn't meant to hurt him. He had come awfully close himself to pressing the trigger of his Colt, and he certainly didn't mean Silvia any harm. Her shooting him had been an accident, he realized. She hadn't known anybody was around until he stepped out of the bushes and yelled at her, and she had reacted instinctively, whipping around and slapping leather.

That brought up some other questions. What was a schoolteacher doing wearing men's clothes and a holstered gun on her hip? And why had her instincts told her to grab iron and fire when she was surprised?

Longarm figured he had better get some answers to those questions before he did anything else.

Reluctant as he was to raise his head from Silvia's lap, he started to push himself up into a sitting position. She placed a hand on his shoulder to gently hold him down. "No, you must rest—" she began.

"I'm all right," he said determinedly as he moved her hand aside and managed to sit up. To tell the truth, the world spun crazily around him for a few seconds, and his head felt as if it were going to break free of his body and fly off into the sky. But then things began to settle down a little. He swallowed hard, nodded his head, and said again, "I'm all right."

"But I shot you!" Silvia said pitifully.

Longarm lifted a hand and gingerly explored his scalp just above his right ear. There was a line of swelling under his hair that was tender to the touch, and his fingertips were slightly sticky with blood when he took them away. The bullet Silvia had fired had barely kissed his skull, just hard enough to knock him down and out for a few moments.

He forced a grin onto his face. "No harm done. I'm glad your aim wasn't a little better, though."

"I never meant to shoot you," she said quickly. "It is just that you startled me—"

"I know," Longarm said. "I figured that out. If I'd known it was you, I wouldn't have jumped out at you like that. All I knew was that somebody was following me, and I thought it might have been Calhorn or somebody else who wanted to bushwhack me." He frowned. "Come to think of it, why were *you* trailing me? I thought we agreed you'd stay back in Presidio while I checked out things in San Ramone."

Silvia picked up the sombrero she had cast aside on the creek bank, and began tucking her long hair under it as she put it on. "You and my brother and Señor Akin agreed to that," she said. "I agreed to nothing."

"You came after me because you're bound and determined to go to San Ramone?"

She nodded. "It was I who first heard of the stranger there from one of the children at the school. I have a right to see if it was Jack."

"No more so than me," said Longarm. "After all, he's my brother."

"Of course. But you are not the only one who cares for him."

Longarm couldn't argue with that statement. In truth, Silvia cared for Jack Ralston a lot more than Longarm did, because Longarm had never even met the missing Ranger. His concern for the man was the same as it would have been for any other fellow lawman who was in trouble or maybe even dead.

Longarm looked around for his own hat, spotted it lying on the bank, and picked it up. Putting it on was a touchy business, but the Stetson didn't put too much pressure on the bullet graze on the side of his head. He thought about tearing a strip of cloth off his spare shirt and binding it around his head to cover the wound, but that didn't seem necessary.

His skull was taking a beating on this case, he told himself. First he'd gotten hit in the head with a board of some kind, then bullet-creased. If this kept up, his brain might wind up a little mushy. He didn't want that to happen.

He got up carefully and would have offered a hand to Silvia, but she was already on her feet, having uncoiled from the ground with a lithe ease that made Longarm feel a mite old and stiff. He saw her horse grazing not far away, and his sorrel was there too, having returned to the creek to be around people and the other horse.

"You know the way back to Presidio," he said flatly.

"Yes, but I am not going," Silvia replied.

Longarm frowned. "Blast it, can't you see that I don't want you going with me?"

"I see only a stubborn man, like all men," she said. "The only way you can stop me from going to San Ramone is to take me back to Presidio and have Stanley lock me in my room. And even then I will find a way to get out and follow you."

Longarm's eyes narrowed, and he muttered, "Talk about being stubborn." He knew she was counting on him not wanting to waste half a day riding back to Presidio with her, but for a moment he almost decided to do that. In the end, he nodded reluctantly and said, "You can come to San Ramone with me. But if the trail leads farther into Mexico from there, you're going back to Presidio."

"Of course," Silvia said, but from the quickness of her response, he doubted if she really meant it.

Well, he would deal with that when he came to it, he

79

decided. Apples were best eaten one bite at a time.

They caught their horses and mounted up, then left the creek behind and continued on the trail to San Ramone. Longarm was still a little shaky and the motion of riding didn't help that, but he soon got used to it. A drink and maybe a cup of coffee would have made him feel even better, but that would have to wait.

The peaks of the Sierra Grande slowly drew closer as Longarm and Silvia rode on through the morning. From time to time, Longarm checked their back trail, but he didn't spot anyone following them. He was convinced that Silvia's presence was the only reason alarm bells had gone off in his head earlier.

Around midday, Longarm's stomach began to growl, but rather than calling a halt so that they could make a meal off the supplies in his saddlebags, he decided to push on to San Ramone. There would probably be a cantina in the village where they could get something to eat. He didn't explain his decision to Silvia, but she didn't complain about being hungry so he didn't worry about it.

Finally, the mostly flat terrain began to grow more rugged, and Longarm knew they were reaching the foothills. "How much farther to San Ramone?" he asked.

"We should reach it in less than an hour," answered Silvia.

Her prediction proved to be correct. As they approached the village, Longarm saw that the cluster of adobe huts was nestled in a small valley between two ridges. The far end of the valley was closed off by a rocky bluff that rose almost sheer. The more gently sloping ridges had enough dirt on them that the villagers of San Ramone had been able to cultivate them by terracing the fields. This harsh land wouldn't provide much of an existence, but it was better than nothing.

Longarm looked at the fields along the slopes, expecting to see men working in them. To his surprise, the fields seemed to be empty. Everyone had probably gone back to the village for lunch and a siesta, he told himself.

San Ramone itself appeared to be deserted, however.

Longarm's concern began to grow as he realized there were no women and children moving around the streets. He didn't even hear any dogs barking.

Longarm and Silvia rode up to the edge of the village. Then Longarm reined in sharply and motioned for Silvia to do the same. She said, "Something is wrong here. Where is everyone?"

"The place isn't usually this deserted?" asked Longarm. Their voices, even though hushed, sounded unnaturally loud in the silence that hung over San Ramone.

Silvia shook her head. "No, there are always people around."

"Well, there's not now," said Longarm, "so I don't know who we're going to ask about Jack." He started to back the sorrel. "We'd better get out of—"

He didn't get to finish the suggestion. The ratcheting of Winchesters being levered cut off his words, and suddenly the early afternoon sun shone on the barrels of a dozen or more rifles thrust through the doorways of the nearest huts. "No, *señor*!" a voice commanded in heavily accented English from one of the huts. "You are not leaving so soon. You just got here."

The man who went with the voice stepped out of the jacal. He was short and stocky and wore tight *charro* pants like a Mexican, but above the trousers was a loose-fitting white tunic cinched around the waist with a beaded belt. The man's hair was black as midnight and hung to his shoulders, held back by the red band that was tied around his forehead. He carried a Winchester and had a sheathed knife attached to his belt. His lean face was as hard and flinty as the mountains rising above the village.

Longarm knew without being told that he was looking at the half-Yaqui outlaw known as Mendoza.

Chapter 16

Longarm glanced over at Silvia. She was scared, sure, but he didn't see any sign of panic in her eyes and he liked that. The chances of them getting out of this village alive were pretty slim to start with, but it would be better if they both stayed calm.

"No need for those rifles," Longarm said as he looked at Mendoza. "Not after such a friendly invite to stick around."

For a second, Longarm thought he saw amusement in Mendoza's obsidian eyes. Then the outlaw said, "We will keep the rifles pointed at you, gringo. The whiteness of your skin tells us that you cannot be trusted."

Longarm's skin bore such a deep permanent tan that he had been mistaken for an Indian himself in the past. In fact, he was almost as dark as Mendoza. He didn't bother pointing out that fact, however. Instead, he looked around the village and asked, "Where is everybody?"

"Avoiding the heat of the sun in the middle of the day," replied Mendoza, "as anyone except a foolish gringo would do."

It wasn't a normal siesta for the citizens of San Ramone, thought Longarm. More than likely, they were cowering inside their huts hoping that Mendoza and his gang would go away without stealing everything they owned or killing any of them.

"Well, then, what are we doing in the sun?" Longarm said. "There's bound to be a cantina around here where we can get a drink and chew the fat."

Mendoza's eyes narrowed. "You speak as if we are *compadres*," he said.

Longarm met the outlaw's gaze squarely. "I don't know you, old son. You don't have anything to do with the reason I'm here. And I don't see any reason why we have to be enemies, you and me."

Mendoza's lips writhed in a snarl. "You are a gringo," he practically spat, "and you ride in here with a Mexican whore at your side! I hate you and your kind!"

Then he really would be upset if he knew his captive was also a lawman, thought Longarm. He was glad he had left his badge and bona fides in his hotel room back in Presidio before venturing across the border. They didn't mean anything over here, and would have only made him more of a target for trouble.

"Like I said, I don't have anything against you, but there's no call for you to go talking about the lady like that," Longarm said, and his voice was as hard and angry as Mendoza's now. Outnumbered as he was, he could be blown out of the saddle by those rifles at any second, so there was no reason for him not to go ahead and speak his mind. He went on. "I want you to apologize to her."

Mendoza took a step back, as if he had been struck. "Apologize? To a *puta*?"

"There you go again," Longarm rasped.

Mendoza held the Winchester in his left hand and used the right to strike himself in the chest with a clenched fist. "Mendoza does not apologize to weak-blooded Mexican sluts!"

That was the first time the outlaw had come right out and admitted who he was, although Longarm had already figured it out. He drawled, "So you're Mendoza. I've heard of you."

"You have heard that strong men on both sides of the

border tremble in the night for fear that I may come to them and kill them?"

Lord, he was a pompous son of a bitch, thought Longarm. His brain, desperately casting around for a possible way out of this fix, seized upon an angle that might work. "What I've heard is that you're a fella who likes plenty of *dinero*. I know how you can get your hands on some."

"How?" Mendoza demanded.

"Help me find my brother. You'll be rewarded by our family if you do."

Silvia hissed, "Custis! No!"

"What about it, Mendoza?" Longarm pressed on, ignoring Silvia's protest. "You know how us rich gringos are. Willing to spend money to get what we want, no matter what it takes."

Mendoza brought up the rifle. "I could take your life right now."

"But you couldn't buy a damned thing with it."

Longarm knew he was walking on a knife's edge. While it was true that Mendoza was an outlaw with an outlaw's greed for loot, everything Longarm had heard told him that the Yaqui half-breed was even more interested in killing those he perceived to be his enemies, which was just about everybody. Maybe Mendoza would take the bait, and maybe he wouldn't.

After a moment that seemed much longer than it really was, Mendoza grunted and asked, "Your brother is missing?"

"He vanished here below the border several weeks ago."

"I could help you find him if I wished to. No one knows this country better than Mendoza."

Longarm nodded. "Name your price."

Mendoza pointed at Silvia and said, "Her. The Mexican whore."

Longarm stiffened in the saddle, and Silvia gasped. Longarm glanced over at her in what he hoped was a reassuring manner, then turned back to Mendoza and shook his head. "No deal. The gal doesn't have anything to do with the business between you and me."

"We have no business yet, you and I," sneered Mendoza. "You have heard my terms." He centered the barrel of the Winchester on Longarm's chest. "What is your answer?"

Chances were that no matter what Longarm did, Silvia was going to be raped and probably murdered by Mendoza and his band of desperadoes. Still, he could not bring himself to simply turn her over to them. When he glanced over at her again, he saw the tiny shake of her head. Her hand was edging toward the butt of her gun. She wanted to make a fight of it. A futile fight, to be sure, but a fight nonetheless. Maybe, with just the right shaving of luck, one of them could manage to put a bullet into Mendoza before they were riddled by the hidden riflemen.

"Sorry, Mendoza," Longarm said, well aware that he might be speaking his last words on this earth. "I don't reckon we can—"

"Mendoza! *Mi amigo!* Do not kill them, *por favor*."

The gravelly voice came from inside one of the huts. Mendoza looked surprised and irritated by the interruption, but he held up a hand and signaled for his men to continue holding their fire. He turned toward the hut and snapped, "Come out here, Claudio."

Longarm and Silvia exchanged another glance. Neither of them had the slightest idea what was going on, but fate had intervened to prolong their lives, even if for only a short time, and they weren't going to complain about that.

The man called Claudio stepped out of the hut. He was big, so big he had to duck his head to clear the top of the doorway and turn sideways so that his broad, massive shoulders would fit through the opening. His head was bald and scarred, as if he had been in a bad fire. The Winchester he held looked a little like a child's toy in his hands.

"What is it, Claudio?" Mendoza asked impatiently.

Claudio gestured at Longarm and said in Spanish, "I would see this one fight. He is a brave man, and he should be challenged."

"You do not want the woman?" Mendoza sounded astonished.

Claudio's eyes licked hungrily over Silvia's breasts. "Of course I want the woman," he said.

A shudder ran through Silvia's body, but the expression of defiance on her face never changed. There was a lot more to her than a mere schoolteacher, Longarm was beginning to realize.

"But we can always take her after the American has been defeated," Claudio went on.

"And who would you have fight him?" asked Mendoza. "You would crush him like a grape."

Longarm's Spanish was good enough so that he was able to follow the conversation without much trouble. He liked to think that he could put up a decent tussle no matter who the opponent, even against a monster like Claudio, but he had to admit that fighting the big outlaw would be a steep hill to climb. Still, he was willing to give it a shot if it would keep him and Silvia alive longer.

"I was thinking perhaps . . . Emilio?" suggested Claudio.

The faintest hint of a smile tugged at the grim slash of Mendoza's mouth. "The master of steel," he said. "Perhaps that would provide some entertainment."

In English, Longarm said, "I ain't fighting anybody for entertainment, Mendoza. There have to be some stakes that mean something, like the lives of Señorita Gonzalez and myself."

Mendoza and Claudio looked surprised that Longarm had understood their conversation in Spanish. Mendoza said, "You would fight my man Emilio with the *cuchillo* for your life?"

Longarm leaned forward and tried to sound casual. "If I win, the girl stays with me and no harm comes to either of us. *And* you help me find my brother."

"And if you lose?"

Longarm shrugged. "Then I reckon it won't matter much to me what happens after that, because I'll be dead. Right?"

86

"*Sí*, a fight to the death," said Mendoza. "The only kind truly worth fighting."

Longarm wasn't so sure he agreed with that bit of philosophy, but now wasn't the time for arguing. He looked at Silvia again, saw the uncertainty in her eyes, and knew she didn't want him fighting Emilio. There was no other possible way out of this predicament, though.

He nodded and swung down from the saddle. "You've got yourself some entertainment," he said.

He just hoped that he lived through the show.

Chapter 17

Mendoza gave a piercing whistle, and the rest of the *bandidos* emerged from the huts where they had concealed themselves when they saw Longarm and Silvia riding toward the village. They were a hard-faced, ruthless-looking bunch, just as Longarm had expected. The huge Claudio was the largest member of the gang, but Mendoza was still the most frightening.

To Longarm's dismay, Emilio turned out to be a short, wiry, quick-moving hombre with a broad grin that showed off the gold tooth in the center of the upper row of his teeth. He was carrying an old single-shot Spencer, but he handed it to another of the outlaws and drew the bowie knife that was sheathed on his left hip. While Mendoza explained things to him, Emilio smiled at Longarm and traced little patterns in the air with the razor-sharp tip of the blade.

Then, with the outlaws ringing Longarm and Silvia on foot, the two of them rode down the street to the plaza where the village well stood. Along the way, Longarm caught a few glimpses of terrified faces peering out from the shadows inside the huts. The people of San Ramone weren't going to help him, and he didn't blame them. They would remain huddled in their homes until the fight was over and the outlaws were gone.

When the group reached the well, Mendoza motioned for them to stop. Silvia started to dismount, but Longarm said quietly to her, "Stay in the saddle. That way you can make a break for it if you have a chance."

That wasn't likely to happen, and Silvia obviously knew it, but she settled back in the saddle anyway.

Longarm swung down from the sorrel and handed the reins to one of the outlaws. He turned to Mendoza and said, "I don't have a knife."

Mendoza snapped his fingers. Several of the bandits drew knives from their sheaths and extended them toward Longarm. He picked a bowie much like the one wielded by Emilio. The handle was carved bone, the curved hilt brass, the long heavy blade the finest steel. Longarm sensed an air of antiquity about the weapon. For all he knew, it could have been one of the original bowie knives forged by James Black. It might have even been carried by Jim or Rezin Bowie.

Not likely, of course, but it couldn't hurt anything to think so.

Longarm hefted the knife, checked its balance, and found it satisfactory. He nodded to Mendoza, who gestured for his men to back up and form a circle.

The only way out of that circle, Longarm knew, would be to defeat Emilio. And even that might not save his life and the life of Silvia. It was possible that Mendoza might think he wasn't bound by a pledge made to a gringo. In the absence of anything better, though, Longarm was going to wager their lives on the honor of the outlaw chieftain.

Mendoza pointed to Longarm's holstered Colt. "Take off your gun," he commanded.

Longarm obeyed, unbuckling the shell belt and handing it up to Silvia. That would give her a few extra shots if she needed them later on, including one final bullet for herself, he thought grimly. Then he took off his hat, tossed it aside, and turned back to face Emilio.

The little bandit was discarding his sombrero. He was still grinning. He tossed his knife back and forth from hand to hand, showing off his dexterity. Longarm waited patiently until finally Mendoza made a sharp gesture with his hand. Emilio was in mid-toss, but he snatched the knife out of the air with blinding speed and lunged forward at Longarm.

Longarm twisted his body and thrust out his own blade to parry Emilio's lunge. The knives clashed with a pure, bell-like ring, then sprang apart as the two fighters did. Longarm took a quick step back to draw Emilio in, then tried to take advantage of his longer reach by leaning forward and slashing at the outlaw. Emilio ducked away from the blow and instantly changed directions with his own knife, bringing it up toward Longarm's arm. The lawman felt his opponent's blade rip at his sleeve as he darted back. Emilio's knife tore only the cloth, missing the flesh of the arm by the merest fraction of an inch.

A shout of disappointment came from the watching outlaws. They had believed they were about to see their *compadre* draw first blood. Instead, while Emilio was turned sideways and slightly off balance from the missed strike, Longarm kicked him in the back of the knee. Emilio's leg buckled and he almost went down, but he recovered just in time as Longarm rushed in. A sweep of the bowie made Longarm spring back out of the way.

Longarm glanced at the outlaws, wondering if they disapproved of his tactics in kicking Emilio. Longarm had always figured that the only rule in a knife fight was to win, and from the rapt expressions on the face of Mendoza's men, they agreed with him. If he wanted to live, he would have to do whatever it took.

There was no time to look at Silvia. All Longarm could do was hope that she was all right. He put her out of his mind for the moment and focused on Emilio instead. The little bandit was driving in again, his blade darting here, there, up and down and to both sides. It was all Longarm could do to ward off the flurry of thrusts. He had to give ground or be impaled on the blade of Emilio's knife.

One of his boot heels caught on a small irregularity in the ground, and he stumbled. Emilio's eyes lit up with anticipation as he threw himself forward in an attempt to capitalize on Longarm's misstep. Feeling himself going down, Longarm knew he wasn't going to be able to stay on his feet. So he let himself fall backward in the dusty street, catching himself with his left hand as he brought his right leg up. The toe of his boot hit Emilio's wrist and sent the bowie flying. Emilio screamed in frustration and scrambled after the knife as Longarm rolled on over and surged back to his feet.

That had been a near thing. If Longarm's kick had missed, Emilio would have been able to slice open his groin. Longarm was sweating now, from both the heat and the tension of the combat. He used his left arm to sleeve sweat off his forehead before it could drip into his eyes and cause them to sting and his vision to blur. He was ready again.

So was Emilio. The outlaw bladesman had figured out by now that Longarm was quick too. He would have to wear down the big *norteamericano,* cut him here, slash him there, make him dodge and duck and leap until his muscles were like lead and the breath burned hotly in his lungs.

Longarm could read those thoughts on Emilio's face as they went through the outlaw's head. He knew Emilio was right too. In a long, drawn-out fight, the smaller, quicker man usually had the advantage. That was why Longarm wanted to end this as quickly as possible.

The other members of the gang were calling out obscene encouragement to their *compadre.* Emilio grinned broadly so that the sun glinted off his gold tooth. He rushed Longarm, but it was only a feint. Longarm recognized that immediately and took a clumsy step to his right, in the direction of Emilio's rush. Instantly, Emilio darted to Longarm's left and thrust the bowie at his side.

Longarm was ready for that, turning the seemingly clumsy move into a lightning-quick spin that put him on Emilio's wide-open left side. Emilio realized he had been tricked and tried to get out of the way, but he couldn't avoid the tip of Longarm's bowie. The keen blade raked along Emilio's side, slicing through shirt and flesh alike. The outlaw's white shirt was suddenly stained with red. Emilio screamed in rage, and startled, angry shouts went up from the spectators. Longarm wondered if anyone else had ever managed to draw first blood with Emilio.

The wound wasn't a serious one, but it served its purpose. Emilio was infuriated now, and as he launched another attack he shouted curses at Longarm. His moves with the knife were intricate and almost too quick for the eye to follow. Emilio wanted to do more than defeat Longarm now; he wanted to humiliate the big gringo first, then kill him.

Longarm managed to block most of the thrusts, but one of them slipped through and gashed his forearm. The steel burned like fire as it cut him. He ignored the pain and concentrated on warding off the rest of Emilio's attack. He was getting more tired by the second now, and the afternoon sun was beating down ferociously on his uncovered head.

Emilio feinted again and suddenly tossed the blade from hand to hand. Longarm had seen the border shift pulled off with a six-gun before, but never with a bowie knife. He twisted his blade and tipped Emilio's knife aside just before it touched his throat. The two men were close together now. Longarm brought up his left fist in a blow that smashed into Emilio's jaw and sent him reeling backward.

A gun roared, and a bullet smacked into the ground next to Longarm's feet, kicking up dust. Holding a smoking revolver in his hand, Mendoza shouted, "This is a knife fight, gringo, not a fistfight! Next time I kill you!"

Longarm wasn't surprised. Mendoza and the other outlaws hadn't objected to his methods at first, but now, with Longarm unexpectedly holding his own, they wanted the odds tilted toward Emilio as much as possible.

Emilio had caught his balance. Now, as he rubbed his jaw where Longarm had hit him, his lips pulled back in a grimace. "I will cut your balls off and feed them to you before you die, gringo!" he said.

Longarm nodded and said, "Come on if you think you can." He wished he hadn't sounded so breathless when he spoke.

Emilio rushed him again. Longarm parried the strikes, then thrust a few times himself just to keep Emilio honest. He was able to nick Emilio once on the arm, but an instant later he was bleeding from a second cut on his own arm. The sight of Longarm's blood must have boosted Emilio's confidence, because the little outlaw bored in yet again. Longarm had no chance now to wipe away the sweat before it ran into his eyes. His vision blurred despite his rapid blinking. His muscles were reacting more slowly, and his feet and legs seemed to weigh twice as much as usual. As he fended off Emilio's attacks, he tried to back away in a straight line, but he stumbled back and to the right instead. This was no feint. Longarm sensed that he was on his last legs.

So did Emilio. He took half a step back, then lunged forward, aiming to drive his blade under Longarm's rib cage and into his heart.

Longarm flipped the blade from his right hand to his left and pivoted to his right. It was a move born of desperation as much as anything else, but if Emilio could pull the old border shift, so could he, thought Longarm. The fingers of his left hand closed around the handle of the bowie. He swung the knife as hard as he could.

Emilio saw what was happening and tried to dart back, but he was too late. His own blade skittered across Longarm's left side, leaving only a shallow cut. But Longarm's knife, with all the remaining strength of the big man's body behind it, sank deeply into the right side of Emilio's neck. Longarm grunted with the effort of the blow, felt the blade grate for a second on bone, and then the bowie came free, slicing through the rest of Emilio's neck like butter. Emilio's eyes were frozen wide in disbelief as his head toppled off his body and thudded to the street. Blood fountained from the neck of the suddenly headless trunk before it fell over as well. The dusty ground thirstily drank the crimson flood that gurgled out of the body.

Longarm stepped back, hardly able to believe what had just happened. Judging from the shocked silence that gripped San Ramone, the rest of Mendoza's band could not believe it either.

Then Claudio let out a whoop and thrust a clenched, massive fist in the air. "The gringo has won!" he shouted.

Mendoza nodded curtly, expressionlessly. "So he has."

Longarm wiped the bowie's blade on the leg of his trousers, cleaning off the small amount of blood that still clung to it. He didn't look at the dead man as he handed the weapon back to its owner. The outlaw took the knife, looking stunned as he did so. Longarm turned back to Mendoza and put out his hand. He said, "I reckon we've got a deal?"

His fate and the fate of Silvia Gonzalez was still hanging in the air, Longarm knew. That made the wait excruciating as Mendoza just stood there and stared coldly at him, saying nothing. But finally the half-breed jerked his head in another brusque nod.

"I will not shake hands with a gringo," said Mendoza, "but I will keep my bargain. You and the girl will come to no harm."

"And you'll help me find my brother?" Longarm prodded as he lowered his hand. Sometimes pushing your luck got a fella killed, but sometimes it worked.

"We will find your brother," Mendoza said. He turned away, clearly dismissing Longarm.

That was all right, thought Longarm. Being ignored was a whole heap better than being killed.

Claudio stepped forward and swung an arm, slapping Longarm in the back with a big hand and staggering him. "It was a good fight, gringo," he declared. "I never thought I would see anyone best Emilio, let alone behead him. The look on his face . . ." The huge, hideously scarred outlaw threw back his head and let out a roar of laughter. He slipped his arm around Longarm's shoulders. "Come with me, and bring the girl with you. We will have a drink together."

Considering the circumstances, Longarm figured that was probably the best offer he'd had all day.

Chapter 18

No one objected when Silvia gave Longarm his holstered Colt and shell belt. Longarm felt a little better once he had buckled on the gun. He supposed that Mendoza figured he and Silvia weren't a real threat, even armed, as outnumbered as they were.

Claudio led the way down the street to a cantina. The group entered the thick-walled adobe building, and while the other *bandidos* went to the bar and shouted for tequila and mescal and *cerveza,* Claudio steered Longarm and Silvia toward one of the rough-hewn tables scattered around the hard-packed dirt floor. Mendoza went with them.

"Sit down, my friends," Claudio said in his booming voice. "We will drink."

Longarm was beginning to understand that Claudio must be Mendoza's second in command. Otherwise he would not give orders so easily. For the moment, Mendoza was willing to allow his *segundo* to take the lead. That could change any time, though, Longarm reminded himself.

A short, stocky man whose mustachioed face was covered with nervous sweat stood behind the bar. He was probably the owner of this cantina, Longarm decided. Two women were also behind the bar, one of them middle-aged with thickening hips and large, pendulous breasts, the other younger, slimmer, with a distinct resemblance that told Longarm she was the older woman's daughter. The sweating man and the younger woman began pouring drinks for the outlaws, while the older woman came out from behind the bar and crossed the room to the table where Longarm, Silvia, Mendoza, and Claudio were sitting. Claudio lowered the hand he had used to signal for drinks.

"I thought Luz would serve us," Claudio said with a frown, referring to the younger woman, Longarm guessed.

"She is busy, as you can see," the older woman replied. "I will bring you whatever you would like."

Claudio reached up and cupped one of the woman's heavy breasts through the thin cotton of the blouse she wore. His thumb plucked at the large, dark nipple that was visible through the cloth.

"Bring us a bottle of tequila," Claudio ordered. The woman stood there stolidly while he continued to fondle her for a moment. Then, when he let go of her breast, she turned toward the bar. Claudio reached out to swat her across her ample bottom and laughed. "Bedding this one would be like slipping into an old, comfortable shoe."

Longarm glanced over at Silvia and saw that her eyes were downcast. She stared impassively at the table. He wished she didn't have to endure the indignity of being forced to listen to Claudio's crude comments, but they both knew she would have been going through much worse right about now if Longarm had not managed to kill Emilio.

"Tell me about your brother," Mendoza said, taking Longarm a little by surprise.

Longarm nodded. "Jack's younger than me and has blond hair. He's a good-looking young fella."

"What was he doing on this side of the border?"

"Prospecting," said Longarm, sticking to the story.

Mendoza nodded. "There is gold to be found in the mountains. Not enough to satisfy a man such as myself, but for someone who thinks only small thoughts it might be sufficient."

"Have you seen him?" Longarm asked.

Mendoza shook his head. "I would remember a yellow-haired gringo."

Longarm wasn't sure if he believed the outlaw chief or not. It was still entirely possible that Jack Ralston had ran into Mendoza's bunch and they had killed him. Mendoza was certainly capable of lying about that.

"I've heard that he was seen recently in this village," Longarm said.

"We can find out about that."

The older woman was approaching the table again, this time carrying a tray with four glasses and a bottle of tequila on it. As she set it down, Claudio reached for her again, running his hand between her legs and massaging her crotch through her skirt. Again she endured the pawing with no change of expression.

"Claudio." Mendoza's voice was sharp, and immediately the big, scarred outlaw took his hand away from the woman. Mendoza said to her, "Has there been a yellow-haired gringo in this village in recent days?"

The woman looked surprised to be asked a real question. She nodded and said, "Yes, he was here for a day and a night and then left again."

"When?"

The woman hesitated. In a village such as this, where one day would be pretty much like another, it was difficult to remember exactly how long ago something had taken place. Finally, she said, "A week ago. Perhaps a little more."

"Did he say where he was going?"

The woman shook her head. "No, but when he left he walked with his burro toward the mountains."

"He had no horse?"

"No, only the burro."

Mendoza looked at Longarm and asked in English, "You understood what was said?"

Longarm nodded. "It sounds to me like Jack's in the

97

mountains somewhere. If you'll let us ride out of here, the girl and I will go look for him." He had planned to send Silvia back to Presidio if the trail led beyond San Ramone, but running into the outlaws had changed that. He didn't want her making that ride by herself. Some of Mendoza's bunch might follow her and grab her.

Mendoza shook his head, and Longarm tensed. The half-breed might be about to go back on his word.

"You killed Emilio," Mendoza said.

"It was a fight to the death," Longarm reminded him.

"That does not matter. Now I am one man short. So you must take his place."

Longarm stared across the table in surprise, and then once again Claudio slapped him on the back hard enough to almost knock his hat off. "Is it not *excelente,* my friend?" Claudio said. "Now you are one of us!"

Chapter 19

For a moment, Longarm didn't say anything. Next to him, Silvia looked equally shocked by this unexpected development. Finally, Longarm said, "Me joining up with your gang wasn't part of our deal, Mendoza."

The half-breed shrugged. "I failed to mention that condition. But it makes sense, does it not? You kill one of my men, you take his place." Mendoza nodded. "That is the way it will be." His tone left no room for argument.

Longarm's voice was every bit as hard as he said, "You gave me your word you'd help me find my brother."

"And so I will," Mendoza said blandly. "After you have ridden with us and helped us with what I am planning."

Longarm couldn't help but wonder what that was. Surely, Mendoza and the other outlaws couldn't be up to anything good. However, that wasn't any of Longarm's business. He was looking for Jack Ralston and those stolen Army rifles, and he had already gotten a good look at the weapons being carried by the *bandidos*. They definitely were not the stolen Peabody conversions.

Claudio poured tequila into one of the glasses and tossed it down his throat as if it were water. "You should be honored," he told Longarm. "Mendoza does not allow many gringos into out little group. Only a handful have ridden with us in the past, and they are all dead now."

"That doesn't sound all that appealing," Longarm pointed out dryly. "Sounds like folks from my side of the border don't have a very high survival rate down here."

Mendoza poured himself a drink, sipped at it, and smiled thinly. "We would make sure that you remain alive, Señor Ralston."

At least until they located Longarm's "brother." Then both of the gringos would become prisoners to be ransomed by their wealthy American family while the pretty border-town girl became a plaything for the rest of the gang. Those thoughts were unspoken, but Longarm suspected strongly they were going through Mendoza's mind.

There was nothing he could do for the time being except play along. He nodded slowly and said, "If you've got something coming up, I suppose I could give you a hand."

"The job will take all of us," said Claudio.

"Just what is it you plan to do?" Longarm asked.

"We are going to rob a train," Mendoza said.

Longarm didn't have to take an interest in the scheme. "Where?"

"It runs between Mexico City and Juarez," Mendoza explained, "but we will take it between Torreon and Chihuahua, where the tracks cross the canyon of the Rio Conchos on a high trestle. We will block the tracks at the north end of the trestle so that the train will have no place to go. It will not be able to back up because we will block the tracks behind it as well, as soon as the cars are past."

"This must be a special train," Longarm commented.

Mendoza nodded. "It will be carrying the payroll for the *federale* garrison at Juarez."

That would amount to a lot of money, even with the low wages that Mexican soldiers earned, thought Longarm. He said, "You must have a friend in the paymaster's office who tipped you off."

"My cousin," Claudio said proudly. "If you saw him, you would know right away that he is related to me, though of course he is not so handsome."

Claudio hadn't been handsome *before* the fire that had

100

scarred him, Longarm thought, but he didn't say that. Instead, he asked, "Why do you need me?"

"I want two men for each car of the train," Mendoza said. "It will be necessary for them to make sure there is no resistance from the guards the Army sends with the money or from the other passengers on the train. I know that you can kill when need be. You demonstrated that with Emilio."

"That was him or me."

"Just as your life will depend on how well you carry out your assignment," said Mendoza. "As will the life of your pretty young friend."

Claudio leered at Silvia, who pointedly ignored him. That didn't seem to bother Claudio or make him stop staring lecherously at her.

Longarm poured himself a drink. Silvia still hadn't touched the tequila. "Say we get away with the payroll from the train," said Longarm. "Then you'll help me find my brother?"

"Then we will go to the mountains and search for your brother," Mendoza promised.

Longarm sighed. "I hate to wait that long. The trail could go cold."

"What other choice do you have?"

Longarm inclined his head and said, "You've got a point there, old son. Maybe it won't be too long. Just when do you plan to pull this train robbery?"

"In five days' time. It will take us three of those to ride down to the spot where the railroad crosses the river."

"All right. I just want you to know, though, I don't make a habit of going around robbing trains."

Mendoza regarded him intently. "What *do* you make a habit of, Señor Ralston?"

"Minding my own business," Longarm said.

"A wise habit." An outburst of ribald laughter came from the men at the bar, and Mendoza glanced at them. "I promised my men a chance to enjoy themselves before we ride south. That is why we came here to San Ramone."

Longarm knew the sort of things men like these outlaws

enjoyed—raping, looting, killing. The people of San Ramone were in for a bad night, and unfortunately, there was nothing Longarm could do to stop it.

"Perhaps it would be best," Mendoza went on, "if you and your whore went somewhere and stayed out of sight for the rest of today and tonight."

Longarm bristled again. "Señorita Gonzalez isn't—"

Mendoza lifted a hand to stop him. "I do not care what she is to you, but if she means anything at all, take her away from here. Otherwise you must be prepared to share her."

"We'll go," Longarm said stiffly.

"Claudio, take them to one of the empty huts," Mendoza commanded. "Place guards on the house. I would not have Señor Ralston neglecting his duty to replace Emilio."

The massive Claudio heaved himself to his feet. "Come with me," he said to Longarm and Silvia. "I will find you a good place to spend the night."

Longarm took Silvia's arm as they went with Claudio. At the door of the cantina, he glanced back at Mendoza. The half-breed was still sitting at the table, nursing his glass of tequila and staring straight ahead. His dark eyes reminded Longarm of the cold, fixed gaze of a rattlesnake.

He and Silvia had been granted an unexpected reprieve, he thought, but that didn't mean they were out of danger. Not by a long shot. As long as they were with these merciless outlaws, death would never be more than a heartbeat away.

Claudio led them down the street to one of the huts. The door stood open, and when the three of them went inside, Longarm saw a dark, irregular stain on the dirt floor of the hut's single room. A set of parallel tracks led from the stain to the rear door. Longarm recognized the stain as the remains of a pool of blood that had mostly soaked into the ground; the air still had a faint coppery smell to it that indicated a lot of blood had been spilled there recently. No one could have lost that much and lived. The tracks had been made by the corpse's feet as he was dragged out the back of the hut.

"Here you are," said Claudio. "A palace, no?"

The house was one step above a squalid hovel. It was furnished with a table, a couple of chairs with uneven legs, and a rope bunk with a woven straw mattress on it.

"You will not be disturbed here," Claudio went on. "I will see to that."

"What about our horses?" asked Longarm.

"They will be cared for."

"*Gracias.*"

"*De nada.* As I said before, you are one of us now. We take care of each other, because we are all that any of us have. The entire world is against us, because we are poor men struggling to make a place for ourselves."

Poor men, thought Longarm, who probably butchered this hut's owner because he dared to stand up to them. Poor men who thought nothing of pawing and assaulting women and taking whatever they pleased. For years, Longarm had devoted his life to bringing men such as these to justice— and now he had to pretend to be their ally.

But the important thing was that he and Silvia both stay alive, so they could continue their search for the missing Jack Ralston. And, although Silvia didn't know about them, of course, the missing rifles as well.

"I will see that you are brought food for your evening meal," Claudio promised as he went on. "Other than that, you will not be disturbed. Men will be watching to be sure of that."

And to be sure that he and Silvia didn't try to sneak off, Longarm knew. He nodded to show that he understood.

Claudio leered at them. "Have a good evening," he said.

Then he was gone, and for the first time since they had entered San Ramone, Longarm and Silvia were alone. He turned toward her, thinking that she would probably like to be hugged and comforted.

Before he could say a word, she drew back her small, hard fist and shot it straight into his face.

Chapter 20

The unexpected blow caught Longarm flush on the left cheekbone, and had enough strength behind it to make him take a step backward before he caught himself. "What the hell!" he exclaimed.

Silvia was still coming at him, swinging her left fist this time. Longarm caught hold of her wrist and stopped the punch in midair. She tried to knee him in the groin, forcing him to turn and take the blow on his thigh. He grabbed her other wrist as she attempted to claw him in the face with her fingernails. Jerking her hard against him, he said, "Stop it! Blast it, what's gotten into you, Silvia?"

She was cursing him in Spanish. Her face was only inches from his and her full breasts were pressed against his chest. Under other circumstances, he would have enjoyed the hell out of being this close to her, but not now when—for some reason he couldn't fathom—she seemed to be mad as a wet hen.

"How could you do it?" she gasped in English. "How could you, Custis?"

"Do what?" he demanded.

"Become one of those . . . those dogs!"

"Wait just a damned minute," he hissed, his voice low so that it couldn't be overheard by any guards that Claudio might have already posted outside. "You don't think I've really thrown in with them, do you?"

"Are you going to help them rob that train?"

"Well, I may have to if I'm going to keep the two of us alive, but that don't mean I'm really an outlaw."

"I thought you were a good man," Silvia said between clenched teeth, "but now you say you are going to help men who are even worse oppressors of my people than the government!"

Longarm's jaw tightened in frustration. "Weren't you listening to a thing I just said?" he asked.

"Those bandits are evil!"

"You won't get any argument from me about that," Longarm told her. "But right now they've got our lives in their hands. Not to mention that they may be able to help us find Jack later on."

She glowered at him. "Your brother would not want you helping such men, no matter if it meant his life. He was a good man, just as I thought you were!"

Longarm saw that he wasn't going to win this argument. He would just have to let Silvia cool off and hope that she would be more reasonable later. He let go of her wrists and took a step back, putting a little distance between them. He was ready, though, if she jumped him again.

She didn't. Instead, she turned away so that her ramrod-stiff back was toward him. A stony silence settled over the hut.

Longarm sighed, reached into his pocket, and fished out a cheroot. He turned one of the chairs around, straddled it, and set fire to the cigar. As he dropped the lucifer to the dirt and ground it under the heel of his boot, he told himself that he could be just as stubborn as Silvia was. He would just wait her out.

She was still standing there when he finished the cheroot ten minutes later. She hadn't moved or spoken. Longarm thought about it, scraped his thumbnail along his jawline, grimaced, sighed, and then stood up. He went to her and put a hand on her shoulder. "Silvia?"

Damned if the woman wasn't full of surprises. This time, she turned around and came into his arms as she began to sob, burying her face against his chest.

Longarm put his arms around her and hugged her, then reached up with one hand to stroke her hair. Silvia trembled in his embrace and continued to sob, but after a few minutes of being held, her crying began to subside. Finally, she lifted her head, looked up at him and sniffled a couple of times, then said, "I am sorry, Custis. I tried to be brave, but I . . . I am so frightened of those bandits."

"No need to apologize for that," Longarm told her quietly. "They're pretty scary hombres."

"Especially Mendoza and Claudio," Silvia said.

Longarm nodded his head in agreement. "Especially Mendoza and Claudio."

She rested her head against his chest again and sighed. "Will they kill us?"

"Not if I have anything to say about it," Longarm said firmly. "We'll play along with them—for now. If a chance comes to make a break, we'll grab it."

"I would rather die than have those men take me." She looked up at him again. "Promise me you will shoot me before you let that happen."

Longarm frowned and said uncomfortably, "That ain't the sort of promise I like to make. Let's just make sure it never comes to that."

Silvia hesitated, then nodded. "*Sí*. We must not think such things." She slipped out of his arms and went to the table, sitting down in one of the chairs. Longarm straddled the other one again. "I hate these bandits," Silvia continued. "They think only of themselves. They plan to hold up that train and steal the *federales'* payroll, but only to line their own pockets with stolen wealth."

"That's what bandits do," Longarm said dryly. "Why else would anybody steal a payroll?"

"To strike a blow against the dictatorship of that fiend Diaz!"

"So you think it would be all right to hold up a train if it was for a good reason?" asked Longarm.

"Of course. Did not the American patriots steal on board the British ships in Boston Harbor and throw all the tea they carried into the water?"

Longarm chuckled. Benjamin Akin had done a good job. This young Mexican woman seemed to know as much about American history as Longarm did. She might even know more, considering that his schooling had been cut short by the outbreak of the Civil War.

"I reckon you make a good argument," he said.

Their conversation was cut short by the arrival of one of the outlaws, who carried a tray with several bowls and a stack of tortillas on it. He placed the food on the table, leered at Silvia for a moment, then left. Longarm dug in, rolling one of the tortillas into a cylinder and using it to dip beans, chiles, and meat out of the bowls. He thought Silvia was going to be stubborn and refuse to eat the food provided by the outlaws, but after a couple of minutes of watching Longarm eat, she reconsidered and joined him.

No one came back to get the empty bowls and the tray. As dusk settled down over the village, Longarm lit the stub of a candle that sat on the table. He went over to the door and opened it. A few yards away, one of the outlaws who had been sitting with his back against the wall of the hut sprang up. He carried a rifle, and he held the weapon with its barrel pointing in Longarm's general direction.

"Take it easy, old son," Longarm told him with a grin. "Just getting some fresh air before I turn in for the night."

He didn't know if the guard spoke English or not. From the man's reaction, he didn't, because he just scowled and motioned with the gun for Longarm to go back into the hut. Longarm nodded and went inside, but not before he heard loud, raucous laughter coming from several of the other huts. The bandits were amusing themselves, and Longarm didn't like to think about how they were going about their amusement.

He shut the door, thinking that there was likely another guard sitting by the back door. Getting out wouldn't be impossible, but it wouldn't be easy. Besides, he wasn't sure he wanted to get away. If he and Silvia escaped,

Mendoza would probably just come after them. By pretending to be one of the band of outlaws, Longarm wouldn't have to worry about them for a while, and eventually they might even help him locate Jack Ralston.

Of course, *then* things would get a mite tricky, since there wasn't really any wealthy family to pay ransom for them, as Longarm had hinted to Mendoza. And if Ralston had managed to find the stolen rifles, Mendoza would surely want to get his hands on them too, and Longarm couldn't allow that.

Well, like the old hymn said, further along they'd know more about it, he told himself. For now, he was tired and wanted some sleep.

"You take the bunk," he told Silvia. "Give me one of them blankets, and I'll roll up on the floor over here by the table."

"You cannot sleep on the ground," she protested.

Longarm laughed. "I'd hate to think about how many nights I've spent on the ground," he said. "If I just had my saddle for a pillow, I'd be right comfortable. But I reckon they left it wherever they stabled our horses."

"Take both blankets," suggested Silvia. "You can fold one of them and use it for a pillow."

That wasn't a bad idea, thought Longarm. He took the blankets and made himself a bed beside the table, being careful to keep well clear of the big bloodstain on the ground. Silvia stretched out on the bunk, using her sombrero as a pillow.

"Try to get some sleep," Longarm told her. "I reckon Mendoza will want to leave early in the morning. He'll be anxious to get to that spot where he plans to stop the train."

For a second, he thought Silvia was going to say something else about Mendoza's plans, but then she turned away from him. With her back to him like that, he had a good view in the candlelight of the sweeping curves of her hips and the long, clean lines of her legs in the tight trousers.

Longarm sighed and bent down to blow out the candle.

Chapter 21

Longarm didn't know how long he had been asleep when something awakened him. Despite what he had told Silvia, sleeping on the ground wasn't really all that comfortable, and it had taken him quite a while to doze off. Once he had gone to sleep, though, he slept soundly, in a deep, dreamless state that nonetheless kept him poised on a hair trigger of alertness, so that he could wake up in a hurry if danger threatened. It was a tricky skill to acquire, but his years of carrying a badge for Uncle Sam had ingrained it in him.

His eyes snapped open, but saw only the faint gray of starlight that filtered in through the loosely woven curtains that covered the hut's single window. It was still hours until dawn, he sensed.

Then he heard breathing coming from somewhere close to him. His first thought was that one of the bandits had slipped into the hut to knife him in his sleep. Since they had made a deal, Mendoza would have had no reason to do that, but perhaps a friend of the departed Emilio who wanted to settle the score . . .

Longarm's muscles were tensed and ready to move. He was lying on his back, so he got ready to fling himself into a roll that would take him out of the way of a knife thrust or the sweeping descent of a club.

He was not prepared for the feather-light touch of soft

109

fingers on his face, nor the whispered sound of his name. "Custis?"

He reached up and closed his hand around a slender wrist in the darkness. "Silvia?" he asked, also whispering.

She gasped and tried to pull back, but he held tightly to her.

"What's wrong?" asked Longarm. He could smell the clean scent of her and feel the warmth of her breath on his cheek, and knew she must have crawled over to him from the bunk.

"N-nothing," she said, keeping her voice pitched so low that the guards outside could not hear it, assuming that they hadn't dozed off already. "I . . . I should not have disturbed you."

"You didn't disturb me," he assured her. "If you need something—"

"No!" The word was a frantic hiss. "I . . . I need nothing. . . ."

Then she moaned and came toward him. He tugged on her wrist to help her, and she sprawled atop him, her slender form fitting easily on his more muscular one. Her mouth found his, a bit awkwardly at first because of the darkness, but then their lips fit together perfectly. She kissed him with a desperate eagerness. He used his free hand to stroke her back and then the full, rounded curves of her rump. The fabric of her trousers was taut over the firm, warm flesh.

After a few moments, she lifted her head, breaking the kiss. "I am so sorry, Custis," she whispered. "I have no right. . . . You must think I am shameless. . . ."

"I think you're one of the smartest, bravest, loveliest women I've ever met," Longarm told her honestly. "And when you're in the fix we're in, there's not a thing wrong with turning to somebody else for a little comfort."

She raised herself a little more so that her hands could rove over his chest. "It is just that I have never . . . have never been with a man . . . and I would know what it is like with someone who is good . . . before those . . . those animals . . ."

110

"Hush," Longarm said. "They won't lay a finger on you. I promise."

She was quiet, but her fingers were still busy, flicking open the buttons of his shirt so that her hands could steal inside and caress him. Finally, she said, "No matter what may happen in the future, tonight I want this. I want this for myself, and for you, Custis. I want you."

"I want you too," Longarm rasped.

His eyes had adjusted well enough now to the starlight that he was able to see her a little as she sat up, straddling his hips. His shaft was hard, and she had to be able to feel the erection pressing against her despite the two layers of clothing between them. She unbuttoned her shirt and stripped it off, tossing it onto the table. Then she took hold of Longarm's hands and lifted them to her breasts.

He cupped the heavy globes of female flesh, pressing them together, kneading and squeezing lightly. Silvia put her head back, closed her eyes, and groaned softly as passion filled her. Longarm could tell she was trying to hold back and not make too much noise so that she wouldn't alert the guards outside to what they were doing. As her hips began to move back and forth, rubbing her tightly trousered groin against his manhood, he had to suppress a groan of pleasure too.

His thumbs found her nipples, hard little buds in the center of large rings of crinkled flesh. He strummed and plucked them, and she rubbed harder against him in response. She finished unbuttoning his shirt, and spread it open so that she could run her fingers through the thick mat of dark brown hair on his chest, and then follow it as it narrowed down and led straight to his groin. She unbuckled his belt, and then began to fumble with the buttons of his trousers.

He continued fondling her breasts as she shifted back slightly to give herself more room. Finally, she succeeded in unbuttoning his trousers, and reached inside his long underwear to wrap her fingers around his shaft. Longarm's hips lurched upward involuntarily. Silvia freed his manhood so that it stood long and thick and proud, jutting up

111

from his groin like a redwood. She took hold of it with both hands and cooed like a child with a new toy. "So big," she whispered. "How can all of it ever fit inside a woman?"

Longarm sincerely hoped to find out before too much longer just how it was going to fit inside Silvia. He clenched his teeth together as she began stroking up and down with both hands.

"And how can it be so hard and so soft at the same time," she asked, "Like stone wrapped in velvet?"

Longarm let go of her breasts and moved his hands to her thighs. "We need to get rid of some more of these clothes," he said huskily.

"*Sí,*" she breathed. "And quickly."

She stood up and, with a foot planted on either side of Longarm's chest, skinned out of her trousers and the underwear beneath them. Longarm reached up between her thighs and pressed the heel of his hand against the delicate mound that was covered with thick, dark curls. Silvia seemed to like that. She let some of her weight sag against his hand, but remained standing above him. He turned his hand so that his middle finger could reach back and caress the slick folds of her femininity. Longarm had believed her when she said she had never been with a man before, but if he had needed any proof, the tightness he encountered as he probed with his fingertip was more than enough. Silvia began to tremble as he spread the lips apart and reached deeper inside her.

Her knees buckled. Longarm caught her as she fell atop him. She found his face with both hands and held his head as she kissed him again. Their mouths were open, and their tongues darted in and out, circling and fencing with each other.

Longarm's shaft was trapped between their bellies and throbbing with its need to be inside her. He took hold of her hips and lifted her enough so that when she lowered herself, the tip of his pole found the wet entrance to her female core. She slid down it in little jerks, impaling herself inch by inch on the rigid flesh. The way she took him in was a delightfully maddening sensation, and Longarm had to impose an iron control on himself to keep from spending too soon.

Finally, she could lower herself no further. Longarm had deflowered a few virgins in his day, although the circumstances had to be pretty compelling for him to do so, like now. He knew what had to come next. "This is going to hurt a mite," he told her.

She kissed him again, hungrily, then said, "Go ahead, Custis. You do not dare stop now!"

"I won't stop," Longarm said as he took a firm grip on her hips, then drove up into her. He felt her maidenhead give way before his thrust. She gasped and spasmed, and he hoped her reaction wasn't completely from the pain.

It must not have been, he decided a moment later as her hips began to move again, tentatively at first, but then with more urgency. Longarm slid deeper inside her, spreading the never-opened sheath and filling her with his manhood. Silvia's inexperience did not keep her from falling into the natural rhythm that was as old as time itself.

Now that he was fully inside her, Longarm let go of her hips and moved his hands to the sleek surface of her bare back. He slid one of them up into the thick mass of her hair and cupped the back of her head as they kissed again. Her breasts were flattened against his chest, and he could feel the erect nipples.

He knew it wasn't going to take long. Silvia was flooded with wonderful new sensations, and she had no choice but to let them sweep her closer and closer to her culmination. Longarm felt his own climax approaching. Silvia gasped into his mouth as she began to shudder. Longarm held tightly to her as his hips bucked up and planted his shaft as deeply within her as it could possibly go. The thick white seed boiled out of his sacs, shot up the length of his shaft, and exploded out into her in spurt after scalding spurt. In a matter of seconds, he had filled her hot, clutching cavern to overflowing, and still the spasms shook both of them. Longarm wanted to shout out his passion, but he didn't make a sound. Neither did Silvia. The need for silence seemed to make the whole experience even more intense. Every sense was heightened.

Finally, in a long, slow spiral, they began to come down from the heights they had ascended. Longarm stroked and caressed and kissed her, and she returned the favor, languidly exploring the parts of his body she had not yet familiarized herself with. When he slid out of her, she reached down and tenderly cupped the softening organ in the palm of her hand.

"So much pleasure," she sighed. "I never dreamed it was possible."

That was just the beginning, thought Longarm. Silvia had plenty more to learn about the joys of what went on between a man and woman.

But he didn't say anything. There would be plenty of time for all that later . . . assuming they could stay alive long enough. That was a sobering thought. Too sobering, he decided, so he pushed it out of his head and tugged her back up into his arms.

"Better get some sleep now," he told her as he stroked her hair. "Tomorrow's liable to be a long day."

"Not in the bunk," she said emphatically. "Not unless you come with me, Custis."

Longarm had gotten a good look at that bunk before it got dark, and he wasn't sure it would hold both of them. Even if it did, it would be in danger of collapsing under their weight. "Maybe we should both just stay right here," he suggested.

"*Sí,* I like that idea." She lowered her head onto his chest and sighed in contentment. Longarm held her, and after a few minutes, he both heard and felt her breathing smooth out into a deep, regular pattern that told him she had drifted off to sleep.

That was good, he thought. No telling what the next day might bring, but at least they could face it well rested.

And with the knowledge that, for a short time at least, everything had been right. That was the power of what had transpired between them. Their passion had shut out everything else in the world.

Longarm went to sleep too, his lips curved in a faint smile.

Chapter 22

Longarm's prediction that the next day would prove to be a long, hard one turned out to be correct. Claudio appeared at the door of the hut before dawn, calling out to them in his booming voice to get up and get ready to ride. Longarm and Silvia were given no time to eat breakfast, but neither were the members of the outlaw gang, many of whom were half asleep and miserably hungover and exhausted from the debauchery of the night before. The group of riders left San Ramone as the sun was coming up, and the survivors in the village were no doubt glad to see them go.

At least Mendoza and the rest of the gang hadn't razed the town, Longarm told himself. The village had been spared total destruction, but probably only because Mendoza would want to come back there and loot it again in the future, when the place had had time to recover somewhat from this visit.

Longarm had some jerky in his saddlebags. He dug out a couple of pieces and handed one to Silvia. "Thank you," she said. She was quiet this morning, and Longarm wondered if she was thinking about what had happened between them the night before. She didn't seem upset, just contemplative. And a little nervous, of course, about being surrounded by a bunch of *bandidos*.

Mendoza kept the group moving at a fast pace. The sun rose higher and grew hotter as the morning went on. The mountains of the Sierra Grande were to their right as they rode south, following the edge of the foothills. To their left was the desert. By midday, it would be impassable, but the heat was not quite so bad where Longarm and the others were. Still, everyone was glad when Mendoza finally called a halt. They found what shade they could and sat down to build fires and prepare a meal, then eat and wait until the sun had slid down lower in the western sky.

Late in the afternoon, Mendoza ordered everyone to mount up. Silvia had dozed off with her head against Longarm's shoulder as they sat with their backs against a small boulder. She gave a small cry as she awoke, and Longarm wondered what phantoms had been haunting her dreams. She gave him a wan smile and nodded when he asked her if she was all right.

The group pushed on, pausing when night fell and it grew too dark to see where they were going. Then, a short time later, the moon rose and its silvery illumination flooded over the rugged landscape. Again, the riders swung up into their saddles and started south, guided now by the moonlight.

Silvia was so tired that she was swaying in the saddle. Longarm stayed close to her and kept an eye on her, ready to reach over and catch hold of her if she started to fall. Claudio, who had been riding up front with Mendoza most of the day, fell back so that his horse plodded alongside Longarm's sorrel. He nodded toward Silvia and said, "The little one, she is tired, no?"

If Silvia even heard the big outlaw's comment, she gave no sign of it. Longarm said, "I don't reckon she's used to traveling this hard on the rim of the desert."

"Mendoza could ride all day." Claudio leaned over in his saddle and spat on the thirsty ground. "With that *indio* blood in him, he could probably run all day."

Longarm thought he heard a faint tone of contempt in Claudio's voice when the big man referred to Mendoza's Yaqui heritage. It was just possible that Claudio resented

116

the fact that a half-breed was leading the gang. Maybe Claudio thought *he* would be a better leader. If that was true, it was something that might come in handy in the future, Longarm told himself. More than once, he had been able to get himself out of a tight spot by playing one side of an outlaw gang against another side.

Of course, he wasn't sure he had ever been in a spot quite this tight. . . .

Claudio went on. "You are holding up well, amigo. I can tell you have ridden some hard trails in the past."

Longarm nodded. "I've ridden my share, all right."

"I think you are a very dangerous man, Señor Ralston. You never let the fear in your heart rule over your brain. Some men would have panicked and tried to get away from us before now."

Longarm shrugged and said, "Didn't seem to be any point in doing that. I'd rather stay alive as long as possible."

"And that is why you are dangerous. You will never throw your life away. You will only sell it, and then most dearly." Claudio's fist thudded against Longarm's shoulder. "I will watch you, my friend. Know that my eyes will always be on you."

With that, he rode ahead again to rejoin Mendoza. Longarm waited until he was gone to reach up and rub his arm where Claudio's "friendly" gesture had numbed it. Claudio was big and ugly, but Longarm warned himself not to underestimate the man. Claudio might well be smarter than Mendoza himself.

But if that was the case, then Claudio would be well aware of it too, and again, sometime in the future, Longarm might be able to turn that knowledge to his own benefit.

It was well after midnight before Mendoza called a halt. The horses were unsaddled and hobbled so that they could graze on the scrubby grass that grew in the foothills. No fires were allowed, so the group had to make do with a cold supper. Then they rolled in their blankets to catch a few hours of sleep. Mendoza posted guards, of course, and Longarm knew there was no point in trying to escape. Silvia was too exhausted to travel very far or very fast. They would just have to bide their time.

The next day was a repeat of the first, and the third one started out the same. Even Longarm, as trail-hardened as he was, began to wear down under the grueling pace of the journey. It was worse for Silvia. She was only half-conscious most of the time, and on several occasions during the day, Longarm had to steady her to keep her from toppling out of the saddle. Finally, after one of the times he'd had to catch Silvia before she could fall, he called out angrily, "Mendoza!"

The outlaw chief stopped and turned his horse to wait for them. When they came up even with him, he asked, "What is it?"

Longarm nodded toward Silvia as he reined in. "She can't go on like this. We either have to have a good long rest, or let her ride double with me so that I can hang on to her."

Mendoza pointed to the sorrel, who stood with drooping head. "Your horse is already tired. He cannot carry double for very far."

"How much farther do we have to go?" asked Longarm.

Mendoza shrugged. "Not far. But you forget, gringo, you are in no position to give orders or demand special favors."

"It'll slow you down even more if we have to keep stopping to pick her up and put her back in the saddle."

"Perhaps if she falls, we will leave her there."

Despite the heat of the day, Longarm felt cold. It would be signing Silvia's death warrant to leave her behind, but Mendoza was fully capable of doing such a thing, he knew. "Just let her ride with me," he said. "We'll keep up."

Mendoza shrugged again, and Longarm knew that it meant they had better.

He dismounted quickly and helped Silvia down from her horse. He wasn't sure she knew what was going on, but she cooperated enough so that he was able to lift her up onto the sorrel's back, in front of the saddle. Longarm swung up behind her and put his left arm around her waist. He used his right hand to handle the reins. As he heeled the sorrel into motion again, he muttered, "Sorry, boy." Very much of this would probably kill the horse, but the sorrel plodded on stubbornly.

Late in the afternoon, Longarm saw something unusual in this brown and tan and gray country: the green of vegetation. The line ran east and west ahead of them, and he suspected it marked the course of the Rio Conchos as the river came down out of the mountains and then curved to the northeast to join the Rio Grande near Presidio.

Like everything in the desert, the trees along the river looked closer than they really were, and it was almost dusk before the riders reached them. The Rio Conchos had cut a shallow gorge here with its occasional flash floods, and the trees grew down inside the gorge, which was some twenty feet from side to side. The river itself was only a few feet wide at the moment. The floods came in the spring; by this time of year the flow had lessened considerably. The sides of the gorge were not so steep that the horses couldn't slip and slide down them, although getting down into the gorge was trickier for Longarm because he had to hang on to Silvia as well as guide the sorrel. Soon, though, all the gang had descended, and the horses stood in the water, their muzzles dipped thirstily below the surface.

Mendoza let the horses drink only for a moment, then ordered his men to lead them out of the river. The horses went reluctantly, and in a few minutes the stream, muddied by their hooves, cleared again. The outlaws began filling their canteens and dipping their own heads in the water.

Longarm dismounted and then helped Silvia down from the sorrel. He sat her down on the gravel bar that lined the riverbank, with her back against a slender tree trunk. Then he went to the edge of the river, cupped his hands in the water, and brought them to his mouth. The stream, still fed by snowmelt even this late in the summer, was clear and cold and tasted delicious. Longarm got an empty canteen from his saddle, filled it, and took it to Silvia. She lifted it to her mouth and drank eagerly. Some of the water spilled from her mouth and ran down her throat, cutting lines in the dust that coated her skin.

"From here we follow the river," Mendoza announced. "It has taken longer to get here than I hoped, so we will ride on tonight."

Silvia groaned, and Longarm felt like doing a little complaining of his own. He knew it wouldn't do any good, though.

During the rainy season—or what passed for one in these arid climes—it wouldn't have been safe to make even a temporary camp in a gorge such as this. Too much risk of being swept away by a flash flood that started dozens of miles away in the mountains. Now, though, there was not much chance of that happening. The bandits built a small fire and heated beans and tortillas and fried bacon. Longarm did likewise, and the hot food seemed to restore some of Silvia's strength. So did the shade and the cold water. The rest would do the horses even more good than it would the riders.

Silvia said quietly, "Do I remember . . . you rode with me, Custis? You kept me from falling?"

"You've had a hard time of it," Longarm said with a shrug. "I just gave you a hand."

She reached up and touched his cheek, which was covered with three days' growth of beard. "You look like a *bandido* yourself," she said quietly, "but I know what a good man you are. I am sorry for all the things I said that night back in San Ramone."

Longarm grinned. "Not all of them, I hope."

Even in the gathering dusk, he saw the warm flush spread across her face. "No, not all of them," she whispered.

Since it was close to nightfall, Mendoza allowed them to rest until the moon rose. Then, slowly, everyone mounted up and rode out of the gorge. They turned west, following the course of the river as it curved up into the mountains. They had to go slower now because the terrain was more rugged, but still Mendoza kept pushing on. The chill in the air deepened as the night went on and the riders climbed to higher elevations. The peaks began to thrust up higher around them, silver and black monoliths in the moonlight.

Finally, Mendoza called a halt as they came out onto a tableland with a much deeper gorge cut across it by the Rio Conchos. Longarm figured it was at least a hundred feet deep. Up ahead he saw the moonlight glinting on steel rails where the railroad crossed the gorge on a narrow trestle.

"There," Mendoza said. "There is where we will stop the train and become rich men."

Chapter 23

By the light of a new day, Longarm got a good look at the layout and knew that what Mendoza planned could be done.

The railroad tracks came up from the south through a narrow cut in the mountains before arrowing straight across the tableland. A few well-placed casks of blasting powder would bring down an avalanche that would close that cut behind a train. The trestle itself was about a hundred yards long. If the tracks were blocked at the north end of the trestle, and the cut to the south was closed, a train would have no place to go. Depending on the number of cars in the train, it might even be stranded on the trestle itself.

Mendoza had the blasting powder. Longarm had seen the casks strapped to one of the gang's pack mules. Blocking the tracks might be a little more difficult, but it could be done in any of several ways.

Mendoza chose to have his men climb into the mountains and chop down some trees so that they could build a barricade across the tracks. Longarm listened to the half-breed give the orders, then shook his head.

Mendoza saw the gesture and glared at him. "You do not like my plan?" he demanded of Longarm.

Casually, Longarm took out a cheroot and lit it. "It

might work," he admitted after he'd blown out a cloud of smoke. "But if the engineer spots the barricade too soon, he'll be able to stop and reverse before he ever gets to the trestle."

"The rock slide behind the train will stop it."

"Yeah, but it's liable to fall down right on top of the train if it's still in that cut," Longarm pointed out. "Then you'd have a hell of a job digging out that payroll from under a few hundred tons of boulders."

Claudio said, "You sound like you have a better idea, amigo."

Longarm pointed to the casks of blasting powder. "You won't need that much powder to start an avalanche. Why don't you put one cask on the rails just past the north end and blow it just as the locomotive starts out onto the trestle. The engineer will probably be able to stop in time to keep the train from derailing—because you don't want it falling into the gorge either—but by then the end of the train will be clear of the rock slide."

Claudio nodded, looked at Mendoza, and said, "It sounds like a good idea."

Mendoza was still scowling. He didn't like Longarm questioning him, and he liked it even less that Claudio approved of what Longarm had said. Some of the other *bandidos* were nodding their heads in agreement too.

"Who will set off the charge on the tracks?" demanded Mendoza.

Longarm shifted the cheroot from one side of his mouth to the other and said, "I reckon I could. All it'd take is a shot or two from a rifle."

Mendoza nodded curtly. "That will be your job then, gringo. But if you fail . . . I will flay the skin from your body and enjoy every second of your screams."

Longarm shrugged to show that he was willing to take that chance.

He felt eyes on him, and looked over to see Silvia watching him. She was frowning, and he wondered if she was rethinking her assessment of him. Maybe the fact that he was cooperating with Mendoza would cause her to go back to her original opinion of him, the one that had prompted her to slug him in the face in anger. Longarm hoped that wasn't the case, but it couldn't be helped. He wanted to save as many lives as possible, and in order to do that, the train holdup had to go off smoothly. In a fight, the men most likely to be killed would be the *federales* who were guarding the payroll, and while Longarm had no great affection for Presidente Diaz's soldier boys, he didn't want to see them massacred either.

"The train will be here early tomorrow morning," Mendoza went on. "We will be ready for it."

Silvia was quiet and distracted all day, barely replying whenever Longarm spoke to her. He kept an eye on her to make sure that none of the bandits bothered her, but much of his time was spent with Claudio, who had appointed himself the supervisor of the attempt to blow up the railroad tracks. His massive hands worked with surprising delicacy as he picked the proper place for the blasting powder and then tied the cask to the rail, nestling it down between the ties so that it would not be very noticeable. That would give Longarm a smaller target to shoot at, however, and Claudio asked him worriedly, "Are you sure you can hit it, amigo?"

Longarm nodded confidently. "I can make the shot."

During the day, other members of the gang, under Mendoza's supervision, placed the blasting powder on the slopes above the cut where the tracks ran. Mendoza marshaled his forces like a general, Longarm thought as he watched the half-breed point out the places where his men would hide until it was time for them to rush the train. By nightfall, everyone knew where he was supposed to be and what his job was when the robbery began. Longarm had no doubt that the gang would be able to pull it off.

That night, they made their camp in a clearing in some brush next to a beetling bluff at the edge of the tableland. Longarm took Silvia a plate of beans and carried one for himself. He sat down beside her and began to eat. After a few minutes, he noticed that she wasn't eating.

"Not hungry?" he asked.

She shook her head but said nothing.

"None of this bunch bothered you today, did they?"

"They have their orders from Mendoza," she said dully. "As do you."

Longarm frowned. "Mendoza's going to help us find Jack."

"After he robs that train."

"What do you care if some of Diaz's money gets stolen?" asked Longarm.

Silvia grimaced. "I care nothing for Diaz!" she said. "He is an evil man and should be chased from the presidential palace with a cat-of-nine-tails!"

Longarm had to smile at that image. He didn't disagree with her about El Presidente. Lowering his voice so that he wouldn't be overheard, he said, "I don't like Mendoza or any of this bunch any more than you do, Silvia, but for now we have to play along with them."

She sighed. "Yes, I suppose. I just cannot stop thinking of how much good that money could do if it was in the hands of someone other than either Diaz or Mendoza."

"Like the Children of Liberty?"

She looked sharply at him. "Why do you mention them? My brother and Señor Akin told you, they do not exist."

"But if they did, they'd put that money to good use, wouldn't they?" Longarm persisted.

"Anything that helps bring freedom to the people of Mexico is a good thing," Silvia said. Her gaze was intense now as she looked at him.

"Sure. Even stealing some old U.S. Army rifles."

She shook her head and said, "I know nothing of that."

"Didn't figure you would," Longarm lied. He had pushed this far enough for now, he decided. He picked up the plate she had set aside and held it out toward her. "You'll feel better if you eat something."

"Oh, all right." Silvia took the beans and began eating.

The air in the camp was tense with anticipation. The

outlaws talked and laughed nervously. They would have gotten drunk if Mendoza had permitted it, but he had ordered them not to swig down any tequila tonight.

Longarm, on the other hand, lit a cheroot and smoked placidly, knowing there was nothing he could do now to stop things from playing out in the morning. Whatever happened would happen, and he would just have to make the best of it.

He and Silvia were sitting near the base of the bluff. She dozed next to him as he smoked. The night grew colder, so he got a blanket and spread it around her shoulders. She snuggled into it, then held it out and looked invitingly at him. Longarm grinned and wrapped himself in the blanket as well. Surrounded by outlaws like this, they couldn't indulge in any slap-and-tickle, but it felt good just being close to her. He tipped his hat down over his eyes and allowed drowsiness to overtake him.

He came awake sometime later when Silvia shifted around. Opening his eyes, Longarm muttered, "What . . . ?" then started to come to his feet as he realized that he was alone in the blanket. Silvia was gone.

Then suddenly she was there, looming over him in the darkness, and he heard her whisper, "I am sorry, Custis," before something slammed into the back of his head and drove him deeper into a blackness darker than any Mexican night.

Chapter 24

Longarm regained consciousness to the sound of Mendoza cursing bitterly in Spanish. He wasn't sure there were any curse words in the Yaqui language; there weren't in many of the Indian tongues.

That irrelevant thought flitted through his aching brain. He sat up and said fervently, "Damn it, I wish people would stop clouting me on the head!"

Mendoza swung around toward him and lifted a rifle, and for a second Longarm thought the half-breed was going to shoot him. It was not yet dawn, and in the darkness Longarm couldn't see Mendoza's face very well, but there was no mistaking the murderous attitude of the outlaw chief.

Claudio stepped forward from the group of men standing around Mendoza. "Where is the girl?" he demanded fiercely.

Longarm didn't mind that Claudio sounded mad at him. For the moment, it was enough that the big man was standing between him and Mendoza. Longarm put a hand to his head, tentatively touched the lump he felt there, and said, "How the hell should I know? She knocked me out before she took off."

"That is not all she did," said Claudio. "Pablo is dead. His throat was cut while he was standing guard."

Mendoza shouldered Claudio aside. "How do we know you did not kill Pablo?" he demanded.

"I've been out cold," Longarm pointed out.

"This is true," Claudio admitted grudgingly. "I myself saw Señor Ralston lying there unconscious, just before Pablo's body was discovered."

"Am I to believe then," asked Mendoza, "that a mewling *woman* killed one of my men?"

Claudio's massive shoulders rose and fell. "She is gone, is she not? And no one else was here."

Longarm knew that wasn't true. Silvia had been in front of him when he was knocked out, and the blow had come from behind him. But these outlaws didn't have to know that somebody else was lurking around in the vicinity.

Several days earlier, an idea had formed in Longarm's mind, and he had been waiting ever since then to see if it was going to come to fruition. Now it was beginning to look as if it might.

But in the meantime, there was still a train to hold up.

He got to his feet and looked up at the stars. They told him it was only an hour or so until dawn. Already the gray of false dawn was seeping into the sky. "You can track down the girl later," he said to Mendoza and Claudio. "It shouldn't be too hard. Anyway, where's she going to go in these mountains? It's pretty much wilderness all the way to Chihuahua."

Claudio nodded slowly. "Señor Ralston is right. We will deal with the girl once we have finished our business with El Presidente's payroll train, no?"

For a moment, Mendoza was silent. Then he said in a quiet, dangerous voice, "I do not like how you always take the side of this gringo, Claudio. When the business with the train is finished, we will talk, you and I."

"I want only what is best for our band, Mendoza," replied Claudio in an equally ominous tone. The showdown between the two men that Longarm had sensed earlier was coming, and sooner rather than later. But not until they had the gold coins from the train.

Mendoza turned away, saying, "It is too late to go back

128

to sleep. The train will be here not long after sunrise. We will be ready."

He gave brisk orders that soon had the outlaws breaking camp. Longarm got his Winchester and checked to make sure it was fully loaded. The day before, he had picked out the spot he would fire from when he set off the blasting powder and blew up the railroad tracks. It was on a small knoll that would give him a slight angle down on the tracks. One of the outlaws would be with him, and once the tracks were blown, the two of them would rush down and take over the engine and its crew.

Longarm wasn't surprised when Claudio announced that he would accompany the gringo on this mission. "The two of us, we will make sure there is no trouble with the engine."

Longarm nodded. "That's right." He hefted the rifle. "Ready to go?"

Claudio lifted his own Winchester and nodded. "I am ready," he declared.

Longarm noticed Mendoza watching the two of them with a scowl on his face as they walked out of camp and started for the knoll. Maybe while they were waiting for the train, he could drive the wedge a little deeper between Mendoza and Claudio, Longarm thought.

They climbed the knoll and settled down to wait. Overhead, the sky had grown lighter, and it was getting harder to see the stars. With the approach of dawn, the heavens took on a hue of gunmetal blue, then acquired a rosy tinge. Longarm took out a cheroot, and Claudio said, "Can I have one of those, amigo?"

Longarm reached into his shirt pocket, saying, "Only got a few of them left, but for a friend . . ."

Claudio took the little cigar and lit it from the same lucifer Longarm used to set fire to his own smoke. After puffing for a moment, the massive outlaw said, "Do not think that because I call you friend you can take advantage of me, Señor Ralston. You are still a gringo."

"I'm not trying to take advantage of anybody," said Longarm. "I just want to stay alive. Whatever problems are between you and Mendoza are your own business."

"Who said there are problems? Mendoza is our leader."

Longarm shrugged. "He's used to having things his own way all the time. There are bound to be disagreements. Just like there are things that you know more about than he does."

Claudio looked off into the distance and puffed on the cheroot. After a moment, he said, "Mendoza *is* an *indio*. I may not look like it, but much pure Castilian blood runs in my veins. My family was once rich and powerful . . . before Diaz seized control of the government."

"So I expect you're pretty well educated," Longarm commented.

"*Sí.* I even went to the university in Mexico City as a young man."

"Yet you take orders from a Yaqui."

Claudio made a sharp slashing gesture. "Enough! You try to poison my mind."

Again, Longarm shrugged. "All I want to do is throw in with the man who's liable to keep me alive the longest and help me find my brother."

"We will see." Claudio squinted into the distance as the sky grew lighter. "If this robbery is successful, we will be rich men. We can afford to help you, especially since you will have aided us."

Longarm nodded. "So we'll wait and see," he agreed. He rolled over onto his belly, took off his hat, and edged up to the crest of the knoll. From there he could look down on the tracks where they left the trestle, as well as back across the gorge to the cut in the mountains where the rails emerged. His eyes narrowed. They might have been playing tricks on him, but he thought he saw a faint plume of smoke far in the distance. From the locomotive of the approaching train maybe?

Longarm looked around the area. No matter how hard his gaze searched the landscape, he could see no sign of Mendoza and the other outlaws. They were well hidden. The men on the train would have no warning that they were about to roll right into trouble.

A man could see a long way in the clear air of these

high mountains. Even though he was confident he had already spotted the smoke from the engine's stack, he wasn't surprised that minutes ticked by with no further sign of the train's approach. A half hour passed, and the sun climbed over the eastern horizon, and still the train was not there. Nor could he see any more smoke. The train must have dropped down into one of the valleys, so the smoke from its engine would not rise high enough in the air for him to see it before it dispersed.

The air had been quite chilly just before dawn, but it didn't take long for the heat to begin building up. The temperature rose along with the sun. Down in the desert it would already be quite hot, and Longarm hoped that wherever Silvia was, she was safe from the heat. Even here in the mountains, beads of sweat were starting to pop out on his forehead. He sleeved them away.

Claudio chuckled. "You are nervous, my friend?"

Longarm shook his head. "Just hot, and ready to get this over with."

"It will not be much longer now."

True to the big outlaw's prediction, within a few minutes Longarm caught sight of smoke again when he looked through the cut in the mountains. Not only that, but he heard a faint rumble. If he had been down there by the tracks, he could have laid a hand on them and felt the vibration of the train's approach. He brought his Winchester up beside him, checked to make sure there was a shell in the chamber, and settled the butt of the rifle against his shoulder. He rested his cheek on the smooth wood of the stock as he lined the sights on the cask of blasting powder alongside the nearer of the two steel rails. The distance was about seventy yards, he estimated, and there was little if any wind. Not the easiest shot in the world, but not too difficult either. He took a deep breath, blew it out slowly.

"Here it comes," said Claudio.

The rumble of the train's wheels on the rails was louder now, and Longarm could hear the *chuff! chuff! chuff!* of the engine too. From the corner of his eye, he saw the locomotive emerge from the cut and roll toward the trestle, but most of his attention was still focused on the blasting powder. He said quietly, "Tell me when the locomotive reaches the trestle." Then he added, "No, just before. We need to allow it a little more time and distance to stop."

"*Sí,*" Claudio breathed. "Wait now, just a moment more . . . get ready . . . *now!*"

Longarm stroked the Winchester's trigger. The rifle cracked sharply and bucked against his shoulder. A fraction of a second later, the cask of blasting powder exploded as the rifle bullet drilled into it. The explosion threw dirt and rocks and a cloud of dust into the air.

In the locomotive, the engineer saw the blast just as the locomotive's cowcatcher reached the trestle. He lunged for the brake lever and hauled back on it as hard as he could, and the scream of locked wheels sliding over the rails hung shrilly in the air.

Longarm lifted his head and as the dust from the blast settled, he saw that the nearer rail was twisted and buckled and torn apart. If the locomotive hit that damaged rail, it would certainly come off the tracks, and if that happened, the rest of the train would topple over and plummet into the gorge. Longarm held his breath as the engine, shuddering against its brakes, slid closer and closer to the end of the trestle.

Two more explosions roared through the still morning air, and a huge cloud of dust rose in the cut as rock slides from both sides closed it off The train's caboose had rolled clear of the cut before the tons of rocks slammed down on the rails. The train couldn't go backward, and it couldn't go much farther forward. Longarm and Claudio came up on their knees to watch as the locomotive finally came to a shuddering stop with less than ten feet to spare before it reached the damaged rail.

"Come on!" barked Claudio. He surged to his feet, leaped over the top of the knoll, and began running down the slope toward the train. Longarm grabbed his Stetson and followed, the Winchester held slanted across his chest as he ran.

They had gone only a few yards when bullets began slamming into the ground around their feet.

Chapter 25

Longarm had expected some resistance from the payroll guards on the train, but these shots were coming from the other direction, he realized. Sharpshooters even higher in the mountains than Mendoza's men were opening up on the bandits as they charged the train. Longarm whirled around as Claudio cried out, grabbed his right thigh, and tumbled off his feet.

Even though some of the slugs were coming dangerously close to him, Longarm didn't want to return the fire. He backed quickly to Claudio's side and bent down to grab the big man's arm. "Come on! We've got to get to some cover!"

"*Dios mio,* what is happening?" Claudio demanded as he climbed awkwardly to his feet with Longarm's help. From the looks of the blood on his trouser leg, one of the bullets had creased his thigh, missing the bone. He was able to run with a painful limp toward the knoll.

The two men threw themselves down as more bullets kicked up dust from the crest of the knoll. For the moment, they were safe from the fire of the unexpected ambushers, but not from the rifles of the soldiers on the train. After a moment, though, Longarm realized that the *federales* weren't shooting. They were probably waiting tensely in the cars to see what was going to happen.

133

Longarm had a pretty good idea. He saw several of Mendoza's men who had been caught in the open by the sniper fire as they charged toward the train. They were down, clutching wounded legs or shattered shoulders. A few were not moving at all.

The pounding of hoofbeats made Longarm glance toward the train. At the far side of the tableland, the tracks entered another cut between stony cliffs. Riders boiled out of that defile and galloped toward the train. They rode like the wind, and Longarm saw that they wore serapes and had scarves wrapped around the lower halves of their faces. They swept up to the gorge, shielded by the engine itself from the rifle fire that was now coming from inside the cars of the train. The disguised figures swarmed past the locomotive, hurrying along the trestle and coolly disregarding the hundred-foot drop so close at hand. Longarm heard shots popping inside the cab. Then the firing abruptly stopped.

Claudio was watching too, and panting a little from the pain of his wound. "Who are those . . . bastards? What are they . . . doing?"

"Taking over the train," Longarm said with a grim smile. He saw serape-clad figures clambering over the coal tender to disappear into the first car of the train. More followed, and the shooting ebbed back and forth, first fierce, then a lull.

"But who . . . are they?" Claudio grated between clenched teeth.

"The Children of Liberty," Longarm said, an admiring tone in his voice.

Finally, the firing on the train died away completely. Occasional shots still came from the heights whenever any of Mendoza's men tried to move out of hiding. The sniper fire always drove them back. Longarm hadn't seen Mendoza since the attack began. If the half-breed was still alive, he had to be seething something fierce right about now, thought Longarm. Mendoza's carefully crafted plan had been utterly smashed, and the loot he had lusted after was being stolen right out from under him.

Longarm had halfway expected as much when Silvia disappeared. He had hoped that someone had followed her from Presidio and that help would be on the way during the journey from San Ramone into the Sierra Grande. Not everything had worked out just right, though. Los Niños had rescued her from the outlaws, as Longarm had hoped they would, but had left him with Mendoza. If there had been time for her to explain, they might have taken him out of the bandit camp too, but to the Children of Liberty it must have looked as if he had willingly thrown in with Mendoza. After all, he had still been armed, and he had spent a lot of time talking to the gang's *segundo,* Claudio.

Longarm would have to wait until later to worry about getting away from Mendoza's bunch and linking up with the revolutionaries, he told himself. In the meantime, he studied the two figures who had remained on horseback while the others in the group took over the train. The big sombreros and the scarves and the serapes hid their features, but the clothing couldn't disguise the proud thrust of Silvia's breasts, or the sloping, rounded shoulders of Benjamin Akin. Longarm wasn't sure how an elderly schoolteacher from New England and a young woman had managed to organize such a well-trained band of revolutionaries, but there was no longer any doubt in his mind that Silvia and Akin were the leaders of Los Niños de Libertad.

A burly figure clambered past the engine with a bulky canvas bag thrown over his shoulder. That would be Stanley Gonzalez, Longarm guessed, and he had some of the payroll with him. Other members of the band followed, each of them carrying a bag of loot. Gradually, the entire group withdrew from the train, mounted up, and wheeled their horses to gallop off north toward the mountains. Longarm grinned and shook his head as he watched them ride away.

"They are stealing the payroll!" howled Claudio. He seemed stronger now. He tore a strip of cloth off his shirt and used it to bind the wound in his leg.

"Yep," Longarm agreed. "That's what it looks like to me too."

"Mendoza will kill them all, slowly and painfully."

"Only if he can catch them," Longarm pointed out. "I reckon it'd be a mistake to underestimate those folks."

Claudio looked over at him. "You called them the Children of Liberty. I have heard of them. They oppose Diaz."

"That's right. They want to free the Mexican people from his dictatorship."

"Bah! Politics! Do they not know that if Diaz is gone, some other despot will only rise to take his place? The only true freedom lies in riches!"

Longarm couldn't disagree with everything Claudio said, but this wasn't the time or the place for a philosophical debate. He wondered if the snipers were still in place on the peaks above them.

There was only one way to find out. Longarm stood up without drawing any fire. He turned to Claudio and said, "Those bushwhackers must've pulled out too soon as the others were clear." He extended a hand. "Come on, let's go find Mendoza."

Claudio let Longarm help him up. They hurried over the knoll, just in case there were still some *federales* on the train who were armed and felt like taking a potshot at something. Once the slope was between them and the train, they headed for the camp under the bluff. That was where the surviving members of the outlaw gang would rendezvous, Longarm felt sure.

Mendoza was already there, and every bit as furious as Longarm expected him to be. "You! Gringo!" he exclaimed when he saw Longarm striding into the camp with Claudio. Jerking his knife from its sheath, he started toward Longarm. "You are to blame for this!"

Longarm turned his Winchester so that it pointed in Mendoza's general direction. "Hold on there, old son," he said sharply. "I didn't have anything to do with what happened out there. I did my job. You saw the powder blow up. It ain't my fault somebody else horned in on your play."

"You knew!" Mendoza raged. "You told them—"

"How, Mendoza?" Claudio interrupted. "Señor Ralston was with us all the time. He had nothing to do with this. It was Los Niños de Libertad."

That brought Mendoza up short. He glared at Longarm. "Impossible! No band of ragged revolutionaries could outwit Mendoza!"

"Reckon you better think again," Longarm advised him dryly. "We all saw it happen."

Mendoza shook his head. "But how . . . ?"

Longarm knew, but he wasn't telling. Silvia had to have told Akin and her brother all about Mendoza's scheme, and they had laid their own plans to take advantage of it. They sat back and let Mendoza do the work of stopping the train, then snatched the prize right out from under him. Somebody in that bunch had some military training, thought Longarm. Maybe Benjamin Akin hadn't been a schoolteacher all his life.

"There is nothing left for us here," said Claudio. "We had better leave while we can."

"The payroll—" Mendoza began.

"The payroll is gone," Claudio said harshly.

"I agree with Claudio," drawled Longarm. "We'd better hightail it. There's a bunch of angry *federales* down there on that train. Maybe they're all disarmed, and maybe they're not."

Mendoza sneered at him. "You think to give orders now, gringo?"

Softly, Claudio said, "Perhaps *I* will give the orders, Mendoza."

Mendoza ripped out a curse and flung himself at Claudio. This direct challenge to his authority could not be ignored.

Longarm could have gunned Mendoza down, but instead he stepped back, knowing Claudio wouldn't want that. The other members of the gang, who had limped and hobbled into the camp while their leaders were arguing, watched stolidly as Mendoza and Claudio came together. Claudio had a knife on his hip and could have drawn it, but instead he met Mendoza's charge with bare hands. Yaquis were some of the best knife-fighters in the world, and Claudio must have known he could not defeat Mendoza in a contest of steel against steel.

Instead, he slapped the knife aside, suffering a cut on his left arm as he did so, and reached for Mendoza with his right hand. If ever he could fasten the iron grip of that massive paw on Mendoza's neck, the fight would be over. Claudio's move was faster than expected, but his wounded right leg betrayed him and he stumbled, allowing Mendoza to twist away from him. All Claudio was able to grab was the shoulder of Mendoza's shirt, which tore away in his hand. Mendoza arced a backhanded slash at Claudio, who barely jerked out of the way of it.

Mendoza's first rush had been sloppy with rage. Now a coldness settled over his face, a killing chill that showed he was back in control of himself. He grated, "You were a good *compadre,* Claudio, but now I cannot let you live."

Claudio beckoned. "Come, little *indio.* I have lived through much worse than you."

Again Mendoza attacked. Claudio shuffled aside, collecting a deep gash in his left shoulder as he did so. He managed to slam his fist into Mendoza's side, though, staggering the half-breed. Mendoza bent over and clutched his ribs, and Longarm wondered if at least one of them was broken. Mendoza straightened, ignoring the obvious pain he was in, and came at Claudio again.

The fight was silent except for the shuffle of feet, the harsh rasping of breath, the thud of fist against flesh and bone, the ugly whisper of knife blade through cloth and skin. The two men circled each other, Claudio as massive and unyielding as a bear, Mendoza as swift and savage as a wolf. Longarm was reminded of his battle against Emilio, but the contrast between the two opponents here was even sharper. And once again his own life depended on the outcome of the battle, Longarm realized. If Claudio went down, Longarm would have to shoot Mendoza and try to grab a horse for a getaway. He probably wouldn't make it, but at least he would have the satisfaction of putting a bullet in the half-breed's vicious hide.

Finally, one of Mendoza's lunges was too fast for Claudio to avoid. The blade sank into Claudio's right side. Before Mendoza could rip it free to strike again, however, Claudio clamped down hard with his right arm, trapping both the knife and Mendoza's hand. Claudio's left hand shot out, and the sausagelike fingers locked around Mendoza's throat. Mendoza's eyes widened as his air was cut off. His shoulders bunched as he drove the knife deeper into Claudio's body, but the huge outlaw's grip on his neck never eased.

Now what the hell was he going to do, Longarm wondered, if they both succeeded in killing each other?

Claudio let out a grunt of effort, and the muscles in his back rippled as he focused all of his strength into his left arm and hand. Suddenly, there was a sharp cracking sound, and Mendoza's head flopped to the side. His body went limp, and his hand fell away from the knife. Claudio stepped back, extending his arm straight out and lifting Mendoza's feet off the ground. He shook the half-breed, then flung him aside. Mendoza sprawled on the ground, dead of a broken neck.

Turning to the rest of the gang, Claudio clenched his right hand into a fist and struck himself in the chest, much as Mendoza had done the first time Longarm saw the half-breed. "Now I lead this band of men!" shouted Claudio. "Does anyone wish to challenge me?"

The other outlaws shook their heads. None of them wanted to incur the wrath of this bloody, battered mountain of a man.

Claudio turned toward Longarm with a tired grin. *"Mi amigo—"* he began.

Then his eyes rolled up in his head and he pitched forward on his face, out cold.

For a long, tense moment, Longarm stood there facing the rest of the gang across Claudio's massive, recumbent form. Then he barked, "Well, don't just stand there, damn it. Help me patch him up."

Several of the outlaws moved to obey.

139

Longarm took a deep breath and thought fleetingly about how downright funny life sometimes was. In a matter of days, he had gone from being a helpless prisoner to grabbing power as the *segundo* of as vicious a bunch of *bandidos* as he'd ever seen.

He wondered what Billy Vail would have to say about that—assuming, of course, that Longarm ever got back to Denver alive.

Chapter 26

Now that he had assumed temporary control of the gang, the first thing Longarm did was quickly patch up Claudio's wounds as best he could. The big man was alive and breathing harshly, but he had lost quite a bit of blood. Mendoza's knife had fanged deeply into his vitals.

Once Longarm was satisfied that he had done what he could for Claudio, at least for the time being, he ordered the big man lifted onto a horse and tied into the saddle. "We've got to get out of here before the *federales* who're left on the train come looking for us," Longarm told the other *bandidos*. He was glad that his Spanish was good enough for him to communicate with them, since some of the outlaws didn't speak English.

They all mounted up. Longarm led them north through the Sierra Grande in the same general direction that the Children of Liberty had gone. The bodies of Mendoza and the other men who had been killed in the fracas were left where they had fallen.

Longarm remembered how Los Niños had gone out of their way to avoid killing anyone during their previous activities. Even today, the snipers in the mountains had aimed only to wound, Longarm believed. At that range, however, and in the excitement of battle, some of the shots had proven to be fatal. He wondered if Akin and

Silvia were upset about that. They probably were, he decided, although the fact that the victims had been merciless outlaws quite likely tempered their reaction somewhat.

Once they were well away from the gorge, Longarm called a halt. He dismounted and had some of the men lift Claudio down from horseback. Now that they had more time, Longarm unwrapped the makeshift bandages and cleaned the wounds with tequila, splashing the fiery liquor onto the cuts from a bottle provided by one of the gang. The shock of the tequila hitting the wounds roused Claudio from his stupor. As the huge outlaw tried to sit up, Longarm put a hand on his shoulder to hold him down.

"Rest easy, old son," Longarm said. "Sorry I had to do that, but I don't want those wounds to fester."

Claudio subsided, nodding wearily with his eyes closed. *"Sí,"* he said. "It is best that the wounds are clean. *Gracias,* my friend." He opened his eyes and glanced around. "Mendoza . . . ?"

Claudio might not remember everything that had happened. Longarm said, "He's dead. We left him back there, not far from the gorge of the Rio Conchos."

"You did not . . . bury him?"

"There wasn't time," Longarm said grimly. "I thought it was better we put some distance between us and that train."

"A wise decision," murmured Claudio. "Still, I have some regret about Mendoza. We had our differences, but he led us on many successful raids. It was not his fault that this one failed."

"Maybe not, but he tried to kill you," Longarm pointed out.

"Sí, he did. There was nothing I could do except settle it between us." Claudio uttered a soft laugh. "So now in my absence, *you* have taken command, Señor Ralston?"

"I just figured we'd better get out of there," said Longarm. "I'm not looking to take over anything."

Claudio shook his head. "No, you are a good man, a

strong man. I would rather have you with us than working against us, even though you are a gringo." He looked around at the other members of the gang. "Señor Ralston is now my *segundo*," he said, putting into words what was already evident. "You will do as he says."

Some of the men didn't like Longarm, and liked even less the idea of taking orders from a gringo. But grudging nods of agreement came from all of them. After seeing what Claudio had done to Mendoza, none of them wanted to oppose him. Just as in any band of wild animals, the strongest ruled.

Claudio lay back and sighed. "Now I would rest," he said. "I am very tired."

"We'll stand guard," Longarm promised.

"And then later," Claudio went on, "when I am stronger . . . we will find the Children of Liberty and take that payroll from them and kill every one of them."

By nightfall, the gang had pushed on deeper into the mountains. Claudio's face was gray with the strain, but he was able to ride. He left it up to Longarm, however, to decide when and where they would stop for the night. Longarm called a halt in a small canyon where pine trees grew around a tiny spring that trickled out of a rocky cliff.

After a hot meal and some tequila, Claudio seemed to be stronger. He sat by the fire with a bottle of the potent liquor gripped in his hand and said, "Those thieves came this way. First thing in the morning, Señor Ralston, I want you to find their trail."

Longarm shrugged. "That won't be easy to do in these mountains. There's plenty of ground that won't take tracks."

He wasn't sure he wanted Claudio and the other outlaws to find the Children of Liberty. If that happened, the gang would try to make good on Claudio's threat to steal back the payroll loot and kill all the revolutionaries, and Longarm didn't know if he could stop them or not. What he really needed to do was find some way to slip away from the outlaws and locate Silvia and Akin and the others on his own. Once he had done that, he would deal with the problem of what to do about the stolen rifles.

For weapons that the U.S. Army had gotten rid of, those Peabody conversions had shot pretty straight earlier today. Longarm was convinced they were what the snipers had been using when they opened fire on Mendoza's bandits.

"Carlos can find the trail," Claudio said, gesturing with the tequila bottle to a narrow-faced, pockmarked outlaw. "He is one of the best trackers in all of Mexico."

Carlos nodded solemnly in agreement.

Longarm had been worried about something like that. "All right then," he said. "Carlos and I will pick up the trail while you rest here with the others."

Claudio frowned, and for a second Longarm thought the big outlaw was going to argue with him. But then Claudio nodded. "It is a good plan," he declared.

And it would work for his purposes too, thought Longarm. He would let Carlos find the trail, then knock out the bandit and leave him there for the others to find later. Meanwhile Longarm would be catching up to the Children of Liberty.

As he dozed off in his bedroll that night, Longarm went over the plan again, and he couldn't see a thing wrong with it.

It was just before dawn when everything got shot to hell.

Longarm came awake at a shout from one of the guards he had posted the night before. His hand went to his Colt and palmed it out of its holster as he uncoiled from his blankets and came to his feet. The bandits who had been sleeping were clawing out of their bedrolls as well, including Claudio, who sat up with a Winchester clutched in his hamlike hands.

A stranger walked into the camp, leading a horse and followed by the rifle-wielding sentry who had grabbed him. Even in the gray predawn light Longarm saw that the man was white. He wore a Mexican serape, but a regular Stetson was pushed back on his thatch of blond hair. With a shock, Longarm realized who the man must be. Only one gringo that he knew of matching this man's description was wandering around down here below the border.

Longarm holstered his revolver and stepped forward eagerly, extending his hand. "Jack!" he exclaimed. "Damn it, little brother, I thought I'd never see you again!"

Now, all that was necessary was that this stranger was really Jack Ralston, and that he picked up quickly on what Longarm was trying to do.

The man stared coldly at Longarm and said, "Who the hell are you? How do you know my name?"

Well, thought Longarm, in this case one out of two really wasn't all that good.

Chapter 27

Longarm summoned up a laugh. "What's the matter, Jack?" he asked. "Have you been wandering around out here in this wilderness for so long that you've forgotten your big brother Custis?" Surely the man would catch on now and realize that both his life and that of Longarm were in danger here.

Claudio frowned in confusion as he looked back and forth between Longarm and the stranger. He had to be starting to wonder what was going on here. He said to Longarm, "Señor Ralston, is this not your brother?"

Before Longarm could say anything, the stranger snapped, "I'm Jack Ralston, but this man isn't my brother. I never saw him before."

Longarm said angrily, "Damn it, Jack, what's wrong with you? Has the sun addled you that much?"

Ralston put his hand on the butt of the gun holstered at his hip. "I don't know who you are, mister," he said tightly, "but I want to know what's going on here. Isn't this Mendoza's bunch? Where's Mendoza?"

So Ralston knew Mendoza? That put a whole new light on things, thought Longarm—a bad light. He'd had the rug yanked out from under him, and now he was going to have to scramble to get back on his feet.

"I do not understand any of this," said Claudio, "but I

do not like it." He moved the barrel of the Winchester so that it was pointed between Longarm and Ralston. "I think both of you should hand over your guns and explain yourselves."

"There's nothing to explain," said Ralston. "I had a deal with Mendoza to lead him to those stolen American rifles he wanted. If he's not here, I'll wait for him."

Longarm's jaw clenched in anger. He still wasn't clear about everything, but Ralston had just convicted himself with his own words. The Texas Ranger who had been so well liked by everyone back in Presidio had gone bad once he was below the border. He had been searching for the stolen Army rifles not because it was his job, but because he wanted to profit from them.

"When did you make this deal with Mendoza?" Claudio demanded. "I know nothing of such an arrangement."

"I spoke with him in Ozona, right after I found out about the rifles being stolen. We got to know each other because he was helping some folks I know smuggle wet beef across the border."

Claudio nodded slowly. "*Sí*, Mendoza crossed the border some weeks ago to make arrangements with some gringos concerning rustled cattle." A harsh laugh came from the massive outlaw. "The fools. When they came across the border we killed them and took their cattle and sold them ourselves. Mendoza thought it was a great joke."

Ralston's hand tightened on the grips of his Colt. "He'd better not be planning to double-cross me like that."

"Mendoza will double-cross no one else. He is dead."

Ralston looked surprised, but he was no more shocked by the morning's developments than Longarm was. Longarm recalled Ranger Sam Horne telling him about how Ralston had been in Ozona working on a rustling case just before the theft of the rifles had brought him to Presidio. Obviously, Ralston was already crooked then and had been working hand in hand with the rustlers. Of course, the wide-loopers had met a bad end below the border, but Ralston wouldn't have known about that.

"Mendoza's dead?" Ralston said after a moment's pause.

"I lead this band now," Claudio told him firmly.

Like most crooks, Jack Ralston was nothing if not adaptable. He shrugged and said, "Sorry to hear about Mendoza, but I suppose I can deal with you just as easy as with him, amigo."

"Do not suppose too much," warned Claudio. "I have no great use for gringos."

Ralston nodded toward Longarm. "You're traveling with this crazy one, whoever he is. He's sure as hell not my brother. I don't even have a brother."

Claudio looked at Longarm, who stood there with a stony expression on his face. "We will deal with that momentarily," Claudio said. He faced Ralston again. "For now, though, I would know more about these rifles of which you speak."

"They're U.S. Army rifles," Ralston said with a grin. "Fine weapons. Once you have them, you can wreak havoc all across northern Mexico. And all you have to do is take them away from a ragtag bunch of revolutionaries who call themselves Los Niños de Libertad."

"The Children of Liberty!" roared Claudio. "Already I plan to kill them all, slowly and painfully! And you say they have Army rifles?"

Ralston was a little surprised at Claudio's vehemence, but once again he was quick on his feet. "That's right. I'll take you to them."

"You know where to find them?" Claudio asked quickly.

"I made friends with their leaders," explained Ralston. "I've been looking around down here for Mendoza for weeks now. I just missed him, coming and going both, in San Ramone."

Longarm's teeth grated together. He hated a crooked lawman even worse than an outlaw. Everyone had been worried about Jack Ralston. Silvia had probably cried her eyes out over him when he disappeared. And all along he had been safe. All along he had been trying to consummate a deal that would put weapons in the hands of as vicious a bunch of killers as was to be found south of the border.

Well, people made mistakes sometimes and misjudged those they thought were their friends. Unfortunately, in this case that mistake might wind up getting Silvia, Akin, Stanley, and the rest of Los Niños killed.

Claudio came to a decision and nodded. "We will honor Mendoza's arrangement with you, Señor Ralston. I want those rifles, and I want those so-called revolutionaries dead." He swung toward Longarm. "Now there is the matter of the *other* Señor Ralston. . . ."

"If I had to guess," said the renegade Ranger, "this bastard must be a lawman of some kind. He came down here looking for me, and he pretended to be my brother in order to give himself an excuse for poking around."

Claudio stared intently at Longarm. "Well, *señor*? What do you have to say for yourself?"

"I say that we are *compadres*, Claudio," Longarm stated boldly. "We have fought side by side against our enemies, and when you were wounded, it was me who saw you to safety."

Solemnly, Claudio nodded. "This is true. But I must know if you are really one of those damned lawmen."

"He's not a Ranger," Ralston put in. "I'm pretty sure of that."

"No, I'm not a Texas Ranger," said Longarm. "I'm not a star-packer of any kind. I heard about those stolen rifles and decided to come after them myself, just like Ralston here. When I heard about him in Presidio and learned that he was missing, it seemed like a good excuse to ride below the Rio Grande, like he said. But it sure doesn't mean that I'm a lawman."

It was a desperate ruse and not all that convincing, Longarm knew, but it was all that was left to him. And Ralston couldn't disprove any of what he had said. Now it all came down to which one of them Claudio was going to believe.

Claudio sighed. "Mendoza would not be fooled," he

said. He nodded toward Ralston. "This man must be a true *bandido* himself, or Mendoza would not have dealt with him. You, on the other hand, *mi amigo* . . . you have been a friend to me, but never have I believed you capable of real lawlessness. There is too much good in you."

Longarm felt his hopes sink with those words.

Claudio looked at Ralston again and asked, "You are sure you know where to find these Children of Liberty?"

"I'm certain," Ralston answered without hesitation.

Claudio nodded sharply toward Longarm and snapped to his men, "Kill him."

Chapter 28

Surrounded by more than a dozen bloodthirsty bandits, Longarm was in as bad a spot as he had ever been. The best he could hope for, he thought fleetingly as his hand flashed toward his gun, was to ventilate Claudio and Ralston before the rest of the gang shot him to ribbons. At least that way, Silvia and her friends might be safe from them. Longarm didn't think the rest of the bandits would be able to find the Children of Liberty.

Before Longarm could draw, a rifle cracked somewhere nearby and one of the outlaws was flung forward as a slug drilled into his back and burst out the front of his body with a spray of blood. More bullets whistled around the heads of the gang as the rifle continued to fire as fast as fresh shells could be levered into its chamber. The *bandidos* scrambled for cover.

Longarm had no idea who was coming to his rescue, but he recalled the old saying about the gift horse's mouth and yanked his Colt from its holster. He snapped a shot each at Ralston and Claudio as he was turning toward the rope corral where the horses were kept. He didn't have time to see if either of his bullets hit its target.

A slug whined past his ear and another kicked up dust at his feet. He kept running. The shooting had the horses spooked, and they were already lunging frantically against the ropes that kept them penned. The makeshift corral wouldn't hold them for long.

Longarm hadn't been counting the rifle shots, but he knew a Winchester held fifteen cartridges. Whoever had ambushed the gang had to be running low on ammunition by now and would have to reload soon.

"Stop him!" Claudio bellowed from behind Longarm. Obviously, the big outlaw hadn't been seriously wounded by Longarm's shot, if indeed he had even been hit.

Longarm reached the nearest rope and ducked underneath it, throwing himself into the mass of skittish horseflesh. That was dangerous in itself. If he lost his footing and fell, he'd be trampled to death in a matter of seconds.

The rope finally gave way, parting with a sharp snap. Freed from their confinement, the horses burst out of the corral and started to gallop wildly along the floor of the canyon.

Longarm jammed his revolver back in its holster. There was no time to catch and saddle a mount. He saw the sorrel he had been riding about to race by him. He darted to the side to let the horse go past, and as it did so he reached up and tangled his fingers in its mane. Kicking desperately, he managed to get his leg over the sorrel's back. Half on and half off the horse, he held on for dear life as it joined the stampede with the rest of the gang's remuda.

Even over the rolling thunder of galloping hoofbeats, Longarm could hear men shouting and the crackle of gunfire. He bent low over the neck of the sorrel to make himself a smaller target, but with all the lead flying around, he would need quite a bit of luck to escape from there unscathed.

For once on this assignment, fortune was on his side. He rode hard toward the far end of the canyon. The outlaw camp fell behind him, and with the horses stampeded, Claudio and Ralston wouldn't be able to mount a pursuit right away. Longarm straightened. For both him and the horse, there was a limit to how far he could ride bareback like this, with no saddle and blanket, no bit, no reins. Luckily, the sorrel was well trained and responded to the pressure of his knees on its flanks.

As he reached the end of the canyon, movement to his left caught Longarm's eye. He twisted his head in that direction and saw a rider slipping and sliding down a long talus slope. The horseman had a rifle in his left hand, and he held it over his head for balance as he tried to stay in the saddle of the wildly careening horse. Finally, with a miniature rock slide right on his heels, the rider reached the bottom of the slope and spurred toward Longarm, waving him on.

Longarm hesitated only a moment, then rode on. This horseman had to be the man who had come to his aid. Now they were both fleeing from the wrath of Claudio, Ralston, and the rest of the bandits.

This morning had certainly been full of surprises, especially considering the fact that the sun was barely up. Longarm had gotten only a quick look at the other horseman, but he had recognized the man. Sam Horne should have been back in Presidio, riding herd on the Ranger post there, but right now Longarm was damned glad Horne, like many Rangers, hadn't paid too much attention to jurisdictional boundaries. Horne must have followed him across the border for some reason, and the Ranger had caught up to him at just the right time.

Longarm's sorrel was fresher than Horne's mount, a big bay gelding. Longarm could have left Horne well behind him, but after the Ranger had saved his bacon like that, he wasn't just about to abandon him. Using his grip on the sorrel's mane, Longarm held the horse back and let Horne catch up to him.

"Go on, damn you!" Horne shouted as he brought his mount alongside Longarm's. "I didn't risk my neck to pull you out of that spot just to have you throw your life away now!"

Longarm heeled the sorrel into a slightly faster gait. He twisted and looked along their back trail. There was no sign of the outlaws. They were probably still trying to catch some of their horses back there in the canyon.

Longarm and Horne had emerged onto a flat, rocky bench. At the far side of it was an arroyo, and beyond that ragged gash in the landscape were more mountains.

Horne kept waving Longarm ahead. The big federal lawman led the way toward the arroyo, and when he reached it, he rode quickly along the brink until he found a place where the sorrel could pick its way down a narrow path to the bottom. Horne was right behind him as Longarm rode down into the narrow defile.

The bottom of the gully was choked with brush. Getting through it was slow. Longarm looked for a way up on the other side, worried that Claudio, Ralston, and the others would follow their tracks to the arroyo and catch them there. It would be simple for the outlaws to sit up there on the rim of the gully and fire down at them. Like shooting fish in a barrel, Longarm thought.

He spotted a possible place where the sorrel could climb out, and urged the horse toward it. The sorrel hesitated, then gingerly placed its hooves on the almost nonexistent path. Longarm was ready to slide down off the horse's back and try to lead it up if necessary.

The sorrel made it to the top, however, and Horne's bay was right behind it. The flanks of the Ranger's horse were heaving from the effort. The bay couldn't go much farther without some rest, Longarm knew. He glanced worriedly back across the bench at the mouth of the canyon.

Several riders emerged from it.

Horne saw the distant horsemen too, and grated, "Damn it! I was hoping it'd take 'em longer than that to catch those horses."

"Me too," agreed Longarm. "Come on." He turned the sorrel toward the slopes.

They had his six-gun and Horne's rifle and pistol. If they had to, they could fort up somewhere and make a fight of it. In the end, the outlaws would probably win, but not before the two lawmen killed several of them.

Maybe Claudio would decide that the cost wasn't worth it.

Not likely, Longarm thought grimly. Not impossible, of course, but sure as hell not likely.

As he and Horne started winding their way into the mountains, rifles cracked behind them, the sharp reports barely audible at this distance. The outlaws were wasting lead. They were still out of range. Longarm and Horne rounded a bend and went out of sight of their pursuers. The respite would be a momentary one, though. As soon as the outlaws managed to get across that arroyo, they could easily close up the distance again. Horne's horse was beginning to stagger.

The Ranger reined in, and Longarm used his grip on the sorrel's mane to bring his mount to a stop. "There's a likely-looking spot," said Horne, nodding to a cluster of rocks. "I'll fort up there and hold them off while you get farther into the mountains, Long."

"You can't beat those outlaws by yourself, Horne," Longarm protested.

"I didn't say I'd beat 'em, I said I'd hold 'em off," snapped Horne. "My horse is done in, but that sorrel of yours is pretty fresh. It can run a good long time yet. I'll give you even more time."

"You'll get yourself killed, is what you'll do!"

"Damn it, don't argue with me, Long!" Horne roared. "You been arguin' with me ever since you hit Presidio. You're the stubbornest man I ever saw!"

"You're a fine one to talk, old son," Longarm pointed out. "You trailed me all the way down here into Mexico, and neither of us have any legal right to be here."

Horne's mouth twisted bitterly. "Jack Ralston was a Texas Ranger. I wasn't going to turn my back on him, not even when some hotshot federal badge stuck his nose into the case."

"So you figured you'd come along and keep an eye on me?"

"That's right. I would've stepped in sooner, but my horse came up lame. Had to trade for another one at some little village. But I caught up in time to hear what Ralston said back there." Horne shook his head in disgust. "I thought he was honest, blast it. Who ever heard of a Ranger going bad?"

Longarm shrugged. "It happens, I reckon. We ain't any of us immune."

"Yeah, I thought for a while you'd really thrown in with Mendoza's bunch," Horne said with a snort. "Then I figured out you were just playin' along with them to save the Gonzalez girl's life." The Ranger frowned. "What's she doing down here anyway?"

So Horne didn't have all of it figured out after all, thought Longarm. He didn't know that Silvia and her brother and Benjamin Akin were the ringleaders of the Children of Liberty.

Maybe there would be time to explain that later. The argument had served its purpose, which was to give Horne's horse a chance to rest for a few minutes.

"We'd better be riding," Longarm said. "Those old boys'll be out of that arroyo by now, more than likely."

Horne frowned as he realized what had happened. He looked down at his horse and then patted the bay on its sweat-covered shoulder. "Sorry, horse," he muttered. "You're going to have to run a little bit more."

Together, the two lawmen urged their mounts into a trot and pressed on into the mountains.

Chapter 29

As the morning wore on, Longarm and Sam Horne tried every trick in the book to throw off their pursuers: finding rocky ground that wouldn't take tracks, riding in narrow creeks, cutting mesquite branches to brush out any marks they did leave behind. Somehow, though, the outlaws always managed to stay on their trail.

That pockmarked *bandido* named Carlos must have survived the fracas when Longarm escaped, and he must be as good a tracker as Claudio had said he was, Longarm decided.

Several times during the morning, the gang came within rifle range. Longarm and Horne had to urge their mounts into a gallop as lead thudded into the landscape around them. Each time, the two lawmen were able to get away momentarily, but the spurts of speed required were wiping out the last reserves of strength in the bay.

Around midday, they were following a narrow, twisting canyon that abruptly ended in a long stretch of high desert. Longarm bit back a groan as he saw the flat land in front of them. The desert was several miles wide, and there was no cover out there. On the far side of it were more mountains, seemingly close enough to reach in just a few minutes, but Longarm knew that was an illusion created by the crystal-clear high country air.

"We'll have to make a run for those peaks," Longarm said. "We sure can't turn around and go back the way we came."

"The gang's not more than five minutes behind us," Horne pointed out.

"Then we'd better not waste any more time palavering." Longarm met Horne's bleak gaze squarely. He wasn't budging until the Ranger did.

With a sigh, Horne spurred the bay into a run.

Longarm's sorrel was tired by now too, so he didn't have to hold the horse back much in order to match the speed of Horne's mount. The only good thing was that the horses being ridden by the outlaws had to be equally exhausted. There was still a faint chance Longarm and Horne could reach the mountains before Claudio, Ralston, and the others caught up to them.

If they did, the cat-and-mouse game would continue, with its probably inevitable results. Longarm hadn't lived this long by giving up, though, and he was damned if he was going to start now.

Five minutes passed, then ten, and the rugged peaks on the far side of the desert didn't look any closer now than they had when the desperate run started. Longarm looked back and saw several dark dots against the lighter-colored terrain. Those would be the outlaws, he knew. As he watched, a few puffs of smoke came from the pursuers. Still wasting bullets, he thought.

Unfortunately, they probably had enough to spare.

So gradually that neither man really noticed, their pace slowed. The Ranger's horse stumbled and staggered and ran gallantly, but it was on the verge of collapse. After several more minutes, Horne realized what was happening and shouted, "Go on, Long! You can make it!"

Longarm was about to reply when something whipped past his head. He knew the sound of a bullet's disturbance of the air all too well. Twisting his head, he saw that the bandit pack was much closer now. They were still at the outer edge of rifle range, but they were steadily closing that gap.

"Go, damn it!" Horne shouted again.

Longarm might have argued, but at that moment Horne's horse finally reached the end of its rope. The bay's front legs folded up underneath it, sending it into a brutal nosedive into the ground. Horne was pitched over the horse's head and landed hard, rolling over in a cloud of dust. Longarm hauled the sorrel to a halt and wheeled it around. He and Horne could ride double.

Horne was already crawling toward his fallen horse. He waved Longarm back with one hand while he grasped the stock of his Winchester and hauled it out of its sheath with the other. Lying flat on the sand behind the bay, the Ranger thrust the barrel of the rifle across its heaving side and aimed at the oncoming outlaws. He began to fire.

Using the horse for cover, Horne could hold off the bandits for several minutes. In that time, Longarm had at least a chance of reaching the mountains. For one agonizing moment, Longarm pondered his choice, then turned the sorrel and kicked it into a run toward the peaks.

If their positions had been reversed, Longarm would have been damned peeved at Horne for not making a run for it. He knew the Ranger felt the same way.

The deciding factor, though, was the knowledge that someone had to find and warn the Children of Liberty that the outlaws were coming after them. Ralston thought he knew where to find the revolutionaries, and given his friendship with Silvia Gonzalez, that was possible. Los Niños was the bigger group, but with surprise on their side, the bandits might be able to wipe them out.

The firing grew more fierce behind Longarm. He gritted his teeth, didn't look back, and kept riding.

Fifteen minutes later, he reached the edge of the mountains on the far side of the desert and began climbing into them. Then and only then did he look back and see that the pursuit had stopped. He heard the faint pop of an occasional shot and saw puffs of powder smoke floating in the air. Horne had made a good fight of it. Longarm was able to see him lying behind the bay, but now he was encircled by the outlaws and they were moving in steadily toward him. In a matter of minutes, it would all be over.

Longarm grimaced, whispered, "So long, Ranger," and then rode on.

By nightfall, Longarm was exhausted, his butt ached like blazes from riding all day without a saddle, and he was hungry as hell. He hadn't eaten anything since the previous night's supper. And out here in the middle of this vast Mexican wilderness, he wasn't likely to find a meal offering itself up to him. There was wild game in these mountains, but the sound of a shot would travel a long way. Now that he had finally given the bandits the slip, he didn't want to lead them to him again.

There was also the problem of finding the Children of Liberty. He didn't have the vaguest notion of how to go about that.

But he was alive, and he still had a good horse under him and a gun on his hip. That might be enough.

He had walked from time to time during the day, giving the sorrel a chance to rest. The horse was still pretty played out, but not so much that it was in any danger of collapse. A night's rest and some good graze would do wonders for it. Longarm could have said the same for himself.

He made a cold camp next to a small stream where clumps of tough grass grew, even at this elevation. The sorrel drank from the trickle of water and began to crop the grass. Longarm drank too, and then stretched out, intending to sleep. The hard, rocky ground and the cramping of his empty belly defeated that intention. He sighed. It was going to be a long, miserable night.

Somewhere nearby, rocks clattered.

Longarm's hand closed around the butt of his gun and pulled it smoothly from its holster as he sat up. Nearby, the sorrel blew its breath out and moved around nervously. The horse sensed something bad.

So did Longarm. A sudden, piercing yowl told him what it was.

Mountain lion.

Well, that made sense, thought Longarm. He had run into just about every other kind of hard luck on this case. Now he was going to butt heads with a mountain lion. He had his Colt, but unless he hit the lion just right, a slug from a .44 wasn't going to stop the varmint in time to keep it from mauling him. The lion, though, was probably after the horse.

The sorrel knew that and let out a shrill whinny of fear. The horse turned to run. In the light from the stars and a sliver of moon, Longarm saw a flash of tawny hide as the big cat leaped over the top of a boulder and launched itself at the horse.

Afoot, Longarm really would be doomed. He couldn't afford to worry now about how far the sound of shots would carry. He tracked the lion with the barrel of the gun as the animal flew through the air toward the terrified sorrel, then began to pull the trigger.

Longarm emptied the Colt in one long, rolling roar of gunfire. The mountain lion twisted sideways in the air and screamed as the bullets drove into its sleek, muscular body. The sorrel bolted just out of reach as the big cat landed on the ground.

The mountain lion was hurt but not down. It pulled itself to its feet and crouched unsteadily as Longarm dumped the empties from the Colt's cylinder and began thumbing in fresh cartridges from the loops on his shell belt. The big cat's tail swished back and forth as it gathered itself for a charge. Longarm snapped the revolver's loading gate closed and lifted the gun. The night air was cold, but his forehead was covered with beads of sweat.

The lion was twenty yards away. It could cover that distance in the blink of an eye. With a snarl that sounded like cloth ripping, the big cat charged.

Longarm only had time to squeeze off two shots. The first one hit the lion in the head but was deflected by its thick skull. The second ripped into the animal's throat as it leaped. Longarm flung himself to the side, but he still felt the fiery kiss of the lion's claws as they raked across his torso.

The lion landed awkwardly, rolled over, and was still. Blood pumped from its bullet-torn throat to form a black pool around its head.

Longarm pushed himself into a sitting position and trained the Colt on the fallen lion, just in case it wasn't dead. He tried to ignore the pain in his side and the way his shirt was growing wet from the blood welling from the gashes. When he was satisfied that the lion was never going to move again, he staggered to his feet and holstered the Colt.

The sorrel! Without the horse, Longarm knew he had no chance of getting out of there alive. He looked around, hoping to spot the animal in the shadows. Maybe it hadn't run too far.

He saw a patch of lighter color against the darkness. Maybe that was the sorrel's reddish-golden hide. Longarm stumbled toward it, calling softly, "Hold on, old son. Don't go running away now."

There was something else, off to his left. Maybe that was the horse, he thought as he turned in that direction. But then he saw movement to the right and veered that way. Suddenly his head was spinning, and he seemed to see a dozen horses—no, a hundred!—standing all around him.

And they were all laughing at him, the dumb beasts!

Longarm opened his mouth to tell the multitude of horses to stop laughing, but before he could say anything, he felt himself falling.

He didn't feel himself hit the ground. He had already passed out by then.

Chapter 30

Plenty of times in the past, Longarm had been knocked out, only to come to later on thinking he heard the voice of an angel. Turned out it was always some gal carrying on over him, and he wasn't dead after all. Sooner or later, though, it was going to be the real thing.

Maybe this time?

"Oh, Custis, I am so sorry. We came when we heard the shots, but we were too late. Please do not bleed to death. You must not die."

Nope, not this time, Longarm thought, and he was actually smiling as he regained consciousness. That sweet voice definitely belonged to Silvia Gonzalez, so he wasn't going to wake up on the other side of the Pearly Gates after all.

He blinked his eyes open and saw her lovely face. Reddish highlights from a campfire shone on her smooth, honey-colored skin. Her dark eyes were full of concern for him, and as she saw that he was awake, she grew excited.

"Custis!" she exclaimed. "You are alive!"

"And kicking," Longarm rasped. His throat felt as if it hadn't been used for a hundred years. He cleared it and went on. "Well, maybe not kicking, exactly . . ."

"Lie still," Silvia said. "You have lost much blood, and you must rest."

He managed to nod. "Where am I?"

"In a camp in the mountains."

"The camp of Los Niños de Libertad?"

Her eyes widened in surprise. "You know?" she whispered.

Longarm nodded again. "For a while," he said.

From where he lay, he couldn't see anyone else, but he heard low voices and the stamping of horses and knew that there was a good-sized camp nearby. He wasn't surprised when another figure suddenly loomed over him in the firelight. Benjamin Akin, looking decidedly incongruous in Mexican peasant clothes, with a serape over his shoulders and a sombrero hanging on the back of his neck by its chin strap, said, "Ah, Mr. Ralston is alive! Excellent!"

"Not . . . Ralston," Longarm said as he felt himself growing weak again. Sleep was trying to overwhelm him. "Name is . . . Long," he went on. "Custis Long. Deputy . . . U.S. marshal."

That was all he got out before he sank back down into the darkness. The Children of Liberty had saved his life. If they wanted to take it now because he was a lawman, then so be it.

Longarm sipped from the hot, steaming cup of coffee and thought about how wonderful it tasted, even without a dollop of Maryland rye in it. He set the coffee aside and had another bite of tortilla and beans. The food was just as good as the coffee.

"You look much better this morning," Silvia Gonzalez said. "I do not think you will die after all."

"Oh, I reckon I will someday," said Longarm with a grin. "But not any time soon, I hope."

"That is what I meant," Silvia said.

Longarm reached for the coffee. "Unless I pass away from sheer joy at how good this breakfast tastes."

Silvia blushed with pleasure and said, "I have received

164

many compliments on my cooking, but never has anyone told me it is so good it might be fatal."

Longarm threw back his head and laughed. That made his side ache a little where the mountain lion had clawed him, but the wounds were tightly bandaged and didn't feel too bad.

It was morning, and for the first time Longarm was getting a good look at the camp of Los Niños de Libertad. It was located in a box canyon that was closed at one end by a sheer cliff, and narrowed down at the other end to an opening so small that a few men with rifles could successfully defend it for a long time. One side of the canyon thrust out so far that its overhang caused a cavelike space underneath it, and this was where the group had made its camp. The other side of the canyon was as sheer and rocky as the cliff face. If someone didn't know this camp was here, he could hunt and hunt and never find it.

Unfortunately, Jack Ralston had a pretty good idea where the place was.

Silvia had admitted that she had dropped hints about the camp to Ralston when he was in Presidio. Unaware at the time that he was a Texas Ranger—albeit a crooked one—she had hoped to recruit him to the cause of the revolutionaries. From the things she had told him, Ralston had been able to make a pretty good guess that she was mixed up with Los Niños, and could speculate as well about where their headquarters was located.

Even though Longarm had told her everything that had happened, Silvia was still having a hard time believing that Ralston had made a deal with Mendoza to help the Yaqui half-breed get his hands on the stolen rifles. She was equally reluctant to accept that Ralston had joined forces with Claudio now that Mendoza was dead. She had to admit, however, that Longarm had no reason to lie about any of this.

Benjamin Akin and Stanley Gonzalez had been talking to the other members of the band, giving them their orders for the day. Now they came over to join Longarm and Silvia under the overhang of the cliff. Some of the revolutionaries would stand guard, while others left the camp to go hunting for fresh meat.

Seeing the members of the Children of Liberty without their disguises had been a shock for Longarm. Some of the young men really were children. Longarm recognized their beardless faces from the school at Presidio, where they were students of Akin and Silvia. Some of them were older, the fathers and brothers of those youngsters. Overall, though, the group hardly looked like a legitimate threat to the reign of El Presidente Diaz.

Still, it was amazing what a small band of people could do sometimes, given enough dedication on their part. And these revolutionaries were nothing if not dedicated.

Stanley had one of the stolen Army rifles tucked under his arm as he hunkered on his heels near the campfire and filled a tin cup of his own from the coffeepot. Originally a Civil War-era musket, the weapon had been fitted with a Peabody action to convert it into a breech-loading, single-shot rifle. Longarm wasn't sure of the caliber, but from the heavy reports he had heard when the guns were fired, he guessed it was probably something like .50–70.

"So," Stanley said after he drank some of the coffee, "you want to take our rifles away from us, eh, Marshal Long?"

"That's why I was sent down here," Longarm admitted bluntly. "Right now, though, I'm more worried about those *bandidos* getting their hands on them. Mendoza's bunch raised enough hell down here without being armed with a bunch of U.S. Army rifles."

"You said Mendoza is dead," Benjamin Akin pointed out.

"Claudio's no better. He's got more education, but he's just as big a bandit as Mendoza was."

"So you want to protect us from Claudio and the others." Stanley looked pointedly at the bandages wrapped around Longarm's midsection. The big lawman's torn, blood-soaked shirt had been burned, since it was beyond salvaging.

"I wanted to warn you," Longarm said. "I've done that. What you do about it now is up to you."

"And the rifles?" persisted Akin. "What are you going to do about them?"

Longarm sighed. "Let's eat the apple one bite at a time, why don't we? Claudio and Ralston are probably on their way here right now."

"I still find it difficult to believe that Jack Ralston could be the corrupt villain you claim he is, Marshal," said Akin. "He seemed like a fine, upstanding young man."

Longarm grinned faintly. "Some folks said the same thing about Jesse James. There's a young fella up in New Mexico Territory named William Bonney who strikes a lot of people the same way—the ones he hasn't gunned down as Billy the Kid, that is. I'd just as soon Ralston had turned out to be on the side of the angels too, but that ain't the way it played out."

"I will believe it when I see it," Silvia said.

"I'm hoping you *don't* see it," Longarm told her. "That's why I came to warn you." He shrugged. "Of course, you found me instead of the other way around, but I reckon it got the job done."

"What do you suggest we do?" asked Stanley.

"Head back to Presidio as fast as you can. Claudio won't follow you across the border."

"You mean we should flee," Akin said. "Run away like craven dogs."

Longarm frowned. "What I mean is, you got to be sensible—"

"Was it sensible for the patriots in Boston to dress as Indians and throw tons of British tea into the harbor?" Akin broke in. "Was it sensible for a small group of men in Concord and Lexington to take a stand against the British Army? The cause of liberty was at stake! Those men couldn't afford to do the sensible thing!"

"This ain't Massachusetts in 1776," argued Longarm, "and those *bandidos* ain't redcoats. They won't come marching along in neat rows just waiting for you to shoot

167

'em. They'll ambush you and murder every one of you if they can do it."

Akin clenched age-gnarled fists. "Not if we strike at them first! Outlaws such as those are almost as big a blight on the cause of freedom as President Diaz and his soldiers. We will strike a blow against them!"

Stanley nodded and said, "*Sí*, we must attack them before they attack us."

Longarm hated to admit it, but they might have a point. The Children of Liberty outnumbered the bandits, and they were just as well armed, if not better. Without the element of surprise on their side, Claudio and his men would be hard-pressed to defeat the revolutionaries. Longarm, aided by a considerable amount of luck, had taken that advantage away from them.

He rasped his thumbnail along his jawline and frowned in thought, then asked, "You reckon you can find them before they find you?"

"This is our land as much as it is theirs," said Stanley. "We can find them."

Longarm wasn't sure about the first part of that statement. The outlaws were probably more familiar with these mountains than the revolutionaries were. On the other hand, the Children of Liberty had found this hidden canyon to use as their headquarters, so they couldn't be regarded as babes in the woods.

He sighed. He could argue it around and around in his head all day without coming to any solid conclusions. What was important was that Akin, Stanley, and Silvia weren't going to be swayed. He could see the resolve on their faces.

"All right," said Longarm, "but you won't be fighting alone. I'm with you until we finish it."

"And then?" asked Akin.

"*Quien sabe,*" Longarm said grimly.

Chapter 31

Scouts were sent out immediately to look for Claudio, Ralston, and the rest of the *bandidos*. The guard was also doubled, just in case the bandits found the hidden camp first.

Longarm spent the day in the shade under the overhang, resting and recuperating from his wounds. It was hot there, because there wasn't much air moving in the canyon, but at least he was out of the sun.

The searchers returned not long before dusk, bringing with them the news that the outlaws were camped a couple of miles away. The scouts had watched the camp during the afternoon, and reported that the bandits seemed to be somewhat lost. Ralston hadn't known exactly where to find the revolutionaries after all, although he had come close. With luck and more time, he probably would locate the camp of Los Niños the next day.

Longarm didn't intend to give Ralston the time.

As for the luck, that would just have to play itself out, one way or the other.

The scouts brought back one more piece of surprising news.

"The bandits have a prisoner," Stanley told Longarm over a cold supper that night. "A wounded white man. They say he is the Texas Ranger from Presidio."

"Horne!" Longarm exclaimed. "I expected Claudio and the others to kill him when they closed in on him."

"Perhaps they are holding him prisoner in case they need a hostage for some reason," suggested Stanley. "Or perhaps they hope to ransom him."

Longarm frowned. "This tangles things up. We got to get Horne out of there before we hit the bandits. They'll kill him right off when we attack if they still have him."

Longarm was surprised, but pleased to hear that Sam Horne was still alive. He had ridden away from Horne once, and that had been a bad moment. The bitter taste of the decision he'd been forced to make was still in his mouth. Now he had a chance to set things right.

"I'll go in and get him," Longarm declared. "Then as soon as we're clear, the rest of you hit them hard."

Silvia protested, "You cannot. You are still weak from your wounds."

Longarm grinned. "These cat scratches? They don't amount to much."

To tell the truth, he knew he was weak, but he sensed that he had already regained some of his strength. It had already been decided in the council of war involving Longarm, Akin, Silvia, and Stanley that the attack on the bandit camp wouldn't begin until just before dawn the next morning. That would give Longarm even more time to rest.

"You should not even be going along—" Silvia began to argue.

Longarm held up a hand to stop her. "I'm going," he said, and his tone made it clear that was the end of the discussion.

"Marshal Long has earned the right to decide for himself," said Akin. "We wouldn't even know those bandits were looking for us if he hadn't escaped into the mountains." The schoolteacher looked at Longarm and nodded. "We all have to strike our blows for freedom and liberty, don't we, Marshal?"

"Don't know that I'd put it in such highfalutin terms,"

drawled Longarm, "but I reckon you've got something there, Professor."

Because he had rested and dozed all day, Longarm insisted on taking his turn at watch that night. Stanley, who was in charge of the camp's security, grudgingly agreed that Longarm could have one of the last shifts before dawn. That way his sleep would not be interrupted in the middle of the night.

So, in the darkest hours of the night, Longarm found himself sitting on a narrow ledge on the side of the canyon overlooking the entrance. He had one of the loaded Peabody conversion rifles beside him, and the chambers of his Colt were full except for the one the hammer rode on. He wore a shirt that Stanley had lent him, because Stanley was the only member of the revolutionary band with shoulders broad enough for his clothes to fit.

Longarm wished he could light a cheroot, but striking a lucifer would sort of defeat the purpose of being hidden up there, he reminded himself. The rock face behind him was uncomfortable as he leaned on it, but that would just keep him awake, which was good.

He was ready for the attack on the bandits. This case had been long and particularly frustrating, and some action would be more than welcome. He liked to think of himself as a peaceable man, but there were times when he needed the heady tang of danger, and this was one of them.

A pebble rattled, and Longarm picked up the rifle and turned toward the sound. His trigger finger relaxed as Silvia whispered, "Custis?"

"Right here," Longarm whispered back to her.

The moon had set, but there was still faint starlight filtering down into the canyon. Silvia used it to guide her as she made her way along the ledge and sat down beside Longarm.

"What are you doing here?" he asked her.

"I came to make sure you are all right."

"I'm fine," he told her. "A little stiff, but that's all."

171

"I am still not sure—"

He lifted a hand and placed his fingertip on her lips to silence her. "The arguing is all over and done with," he said. "In a little while, we'll be leaving. If anybody ought to stay behind, it's you."

She shook her head. "Never."

"That's why I didn't waste my breath," Longarm said with a chuckle.

She caught hold of his wrist and laid his hand against the smoothness of her cheek. He thought he felt the damp trickle of a tear, but he wasn't sure.

"I never thought I would fall in love with a gringo," Silvia said huskily. "Then Jack Ralston came to Presidio, and I believed that was what I felt for him. I know now that was false."

"Silvia . . ." Longarm began. He didn't like the turn this conversation was taking, especially considering the fact that in a hour or two, they would be fighting for their lives.

"Do not worry. I will not say things that you do not want to hear, Custis. But I could not let the sun rise without . . . without being with you again."

She moved into his arms, being careful not to put much pressure on the bandaged-up gashes in his side. Her mouth found his, and they kissed hotly and hungrily for a long moment. Longarm knew this wasn't a good idea. He was supposed to be standing guard, and the sensations that Silvia was creating in him were playing hell with his vigilance and alertness.

But he couldn't help it. He wanted to be with her again too.

It was awkward there on the ledge, but they managed. Silvia began by stroking his groin and then freeing his stiff manhood from his trousers. She stroked the hard rod of flesh for several moments, then whispered, "I have heard the women talk of doing this to their men."

With that, she lowered her head and took the crown of his shaft in her mouth. Her lips closed around it with maddeningly exquisite pressure. Her tongue swirled around the head of his organ and then toyed with the opening, lapping up the clear fluid that was beginning to well from it. Her mouth opened wider as she took in more of him.

Longarm stroked her midnight-black hair as her oral caresses continued. After a time, she took her mouth off his shaft and began to lick all along its length, up and down and around, wetting it thoroughly with her tongue. Longarm thought more than once that his climax was going to explode all over her face, but he managed to control himself.

Finally she rose up and straddled his thighs, pulling her skirt up so that there was nothing between them as she settled down. The tip of Longarm's shaft met the feminine folds and penetrated easily between them. She was already drenched with the need to have him inside her.

She slid all the way down until he was completely buried within her. She put her hands on his shoulders so that her weight would not be on his injured side, then began to pump her hips back and forth. His shaft moved in and out of her hotly clenching flesh.

The urgency both of them felt meant that this wouldn't last long. Longarm cupped her breasts through her blouse, then pulled the neckline down so that they popped free. His lips found an erect nipple and sucked greedily on it for a while before moving over to the other one. While he was doing that, Silvia began to gasp with passion, and her groin thrust harder against his.

Longarm lifted his head from her breasts and their mouths came together again. Their lips were open so that their tongues met, fencing and darting around each other. Longarm's embrace tightened around her. The two of them were so close together they seemed to merge into one.

Longarm's climax was so sudden and intense that it almost took him by surprise. Silvia began to shudder and spasm at the same instant. Thick, scalding fluid burst out of Longarm's shaft and filled Silvia. Longarm's hips jerked up again and again as more explosions shook him.

It seemed to take forever before he was drained. At long last, his organ gave one final spurt and then began to soften. Both of them were soaked with the fruits of their lovemaking. Silvia gave a long, breathy sigh as Longarm's shaft slipped out of her. She buried her face against his shoulder.

Longarm stroked her hair again and held her nestled against him. The wounds in his side ached a little, but he was confident they hadn't broken open and started to bleed again. Even if they had, it would have been worth it, he decided. He hadn't experienced such intense passion in a long time. Silvia Gonzalez was one special *señorita*.

She straightened up, brushed a kiss across his lips, and said, "I will go now, Custis. You have given me what I needed, and no matter what happens this morning, I will always remember you."

"I'll never forget you either," he said, "but nothing is going to happen except we're going to whip those *bandidos* and send them running off with their tails betwixt their legs."

"Of course we will." Silvia stood up, and with a rustle of cloth her skirt fell around her thighs again. "*Vaya con Dios*, Custis," she whispered as she faded out of sight along the ledge.

"*Vaya con Dios*," Longarm said into the darkness.

Chapter 32

Longarm's boots were tied together with a piece of rawhide and slung around his neck. He wore moccasins borrowed from one of the Children of Liberty. Right now, as he stole closer to the camp of the *bandidos,* stealth was the most important consideration.

Claudio, Ralston, and the others were camped in a cluster of scrub pine on the side of a hill. A trickle of water ran down the slope from a spring up above somewhere. The bandits had built a small fire that was mostly concealed by the trees. Now, at this hour not long before dawn, the fire had died down to faintly glowing embers. They cast just enough light for Longarm to be able to see the shapes of the men in their bedrolls and the horses penned in another rope corral strung between some of the trees.

Longarm had circled the camp so that he could approach it from above. As he drew nearer, he knew that Silvia, Akin, Stanley, and the other members of Los Niños de Libertad were also closing in. They had the bandit camp surrounded.

There had to be at least one sentry posted somewhere around the camp, thought Longarm as he flitted from a cluster of boulders to a clump of brush and then crouched down again to wait and see if he had been spotted. He couldn't bring himself to believe that Claudio would be so lax as to not put out any guards.

The scrape of steel on leather as a knife was drawn was the only warning Longarm had.

Out of blind instinct, he dropped to one knee and then dived to the side. Above and behind him, the sentry grunted as he swung a knife with a long, heavy blade through the space Longarm's neck had occupied a second earlier. Longarm rolled over and kicked up, driving the heel of his right foot into the sentry's groin. The man made a little whimpering noise as he dropped his knife and doubled over.

Longarm's hand flashed out and caught the knife before it could clatter against the rocky ground. He reached up with the other hand, grabbed the serape of the doubled-over guard, and jerked him down. The knife went into his throat, forever preventing any outcry. Blood flooded hotly over Longarm's hand as the sentry collapsed. Longarm ripped the blade free from the dead man's throat.

That had been close. If the sentry had been smart, he would have stood off out of reach and gunned Longarm down. Either that, or yell for help. Instead he had tried to kill the intruder himself, probably in order to heap some glory on his head, and all it had gotten him for his trouble was a length of cold steel in his gizzard.

Longarm wiped the blood off the knife and his hand as best he could on the dead man's serape, then stood up and resumed his stealthy approach to the bandit camp.

A few minutes later he was in position. He spotted Sam Horne lying near the embers of the campfire, identifying the Texas Ranger by the big Stetson that lay beside the bedroll. On hands and knees Longarm crept toward him. Raucous snores came from most of the bandits, indicating that they were really asleep. If Horne didn't raise a ruckus, Longarm thought he and the Ranger could slip out of the camp, especially now that the guard was dead.

Of course, Claudio had probably posted more than one sentry. . . .

Longarm was almost within arm's reach of Horne now.

The revolutionaries weren't going to attack until they heard Longarm's signal, a couple of closely spaced shots that would indicate Longarm and Horne were out of the camp. Longarm reached toward the sleeping figure, intending to clamp his hand over Horne's mouth so that the Ranger couldn't make any startled outcry when he woke up.

Another few inches . . .

Longarm's hand came down over the face of the sleeping man, and he hissed, "Horne! Don't make a sound! It's me, Custis Long!"

Suddenly, the man in the bedroll twisted and squirmed and fought like a wildcat. Sharp teeth sank into the skin of Longarm's palm, and might have done serious damage if Longarm hadn't jerked his hand back quickly enough. The man howled as he struck at Longarm and tried to come up off the ground. In the faint glow from the campfire, Longarm saw the pockmarked face of the outlaw named Carlos, who had obviously appropriated Horne's Stetson.

No point in trying to be quiet now. Longarm balled his hand into a fist and smashed it into Carlos's face. The outlaw fell back, stunned.

The other *bandidos* were alerted now, though, and they started struggling out of their bedrolls. Running footsteps sounded nearby, and Longarm knew that was probably the remaining guard rushing back into camp to see what the commotion was.

"Horne!" Longarm bellowed as he flipped his Colt out of its holster. "Horne, where the hell are you?"

"Right here, damn it!" Horne's voice came from the other side of the campfire. The Ranger sat up and lunged toward one of the bandits who was raising a rifle. Horne's hands were bound together in front of him, but he was able to grab the barrel of the rifle and force it down.

"Kill them! Kill them both!"

The roaring command came from a figure so large that it could only be Claudio. Longarm triggered a couple of shots at the massive shape, but Claudio was already mov-

177

ing with that deceptive speed of his. Flame blossomed from the gun he held in his fist.

Longarm heard a slug whip past his head. He fired twice more and saw two of the startled outlaws fall. Meanwhile Horne had struggled to his feet and used his grip on the barrel of the rifle he had grabbed to drive the weapon's stock into the belly of its owner. The bandit doubled over. Horne ripped the rifle free and slammed the barrel over the man's head. The outlaw went down.

Longarm threw his final shot toward Claudio, who was heading for the horses. All around the camp, muzzle flashes split the predawn shadows as the revolutionaries opened fire. Several more of the bandits went down under the volley, but some of the bullets came dangerously close to Longarm too. In this light, accurate shooting was going to be tricky. That was why the fight wasn't supposed to start until Longarm and Horne were well clear. That way the Children of Liberty would have known that everyone in the camp was an enemy and safe to shoot at.

"Come on, Horne!" Longarm called. "Let's get out of here!"

Horne started around the fire, but his left leg folded up underneath him. Longarm realized it had probably been wounded when the Ranger was taken prisoner by the gang. He leaped toward Horne and caught his arm before he could fall all the way to the ground. The two lawmen ran away from the fire. Horne limped heavily, but he did his best to keep up.

Longarm hadn't seen Jack Ralston anywhere, but in the confusion of the attack that wasn't surprising. He felt confident that Ralston had been one of the surprised figures scurrying around the camp.

Suddenly, hoofbeats pounded right behind them, and Longarm and Horne had to throw themselves out of the way of a galloping horse. Longarm went to the right, Horne to the left. The horse thundered between them, carrying Claudio on its back. The huge bandit veered his mount downslope.

Longarm came up on his knees, wishing that his revolver still had at least one bullet in it. Claudio's broad back was a tempting target.

As Longarm watched, a slender figure stepped out from behind some rocks and placed itself squarely in the path of the fleeing bandit. The sky was gray now, with a band of red along the eastern horizon that heralded the rising of the sun. The light was strong enough for Longarm to recognize Benjamin Akin as the schoolteacher tried to stop Claudio's escape.

The horse carrying Claudio bore down on Akin, who never flinched as he lifted the rifle in his hands to his shoulder and fired. Claudio jerked on the horse's bare back but didn't fall. He fired his pistol, and Akin staggered back against the rocks. Akin dropped the rifle but stayed on his feet. He reached under his serape and hauled out an old-fashioned flintlock pistol. Longarm hadn't seen one like it in years. With trembling hands, Akin drew back the hammer and aimed the antique weapon. Sparks flashed in its pan as the hammer fell. The heavy pistol roared.

Claudio's horse was almost on top of Akin by now. The flintlock pistol's blast made the animal shy violently to one side and avoid the schoolteacher. Claudio clutched his chest, tried to stay on the horse, but failed. He toppled off and landed in a heap on the ground.

Akin was down too, having sagged to his knees. The pistol slipped out of his hand. Akin fell forward.

"Damn," Horne said in a hushed voice. "Is that gent that old schoolteacher from Presidio?"

Longarm was on his feet again. He helped Horne up. "That's Akin, all right," he said. "A patriot."

Claudio's horse was still running away down the hill, but Longarm abruptly realized that its hoofbeats were just about the only sound breaking the silent dawn. The gunfire around the camp had stopped, and the members of Los Niños de Libertad were coming out of hiding now and approaching the camp cautiously with their rifles leveled. Longarm looked around and saw that the bandits were all either dead or wounded or had their hands high in the air in surrender.

Longarm and Horne headed for Benjamin Akin. Stanley Gonzalez came running up just as they reached the fallen schoolteacher. "Señor Akin!" Stanley cried in alarm. "Señor Akin!"

Longarm knelt beside Akin and gently rolled him onto his back while Horne limped over to check on Claudio. Akin's eyes were open. Blood trickled from the corner of his mouth. His spectacles were smashed, and the shards of glass had left cuts on his sunken cheeks.

"The . . . the bandit . . . ?" Akin rasped.

"Dead, I think," Longarm told him as he supported Akin's head. He glanced over at Horne, who straightened from bending over Claudio and gave him a confirming nod. "Yeah, he's dead, all right," Longarm went on. "You stopped him, Benjamin. I reckon that makes you a hero, just like your pa back there in Revolutionary times."

"No . . ." Akin clutched at Longarm's sleeve. "Not a . . . hero. My father was . . . a Tory . . . a traitor to the cause . . . of liberty . . . I've been . . . lying about him . . . all these years . . . trying to live down the shame, to make up for what he did." His grip tightened, and his voice grew stronger. "Stanley?"

"I am here, Señor Akin," Stanley replied in a grief-stricken tone.

"You and Silvia and the others must carry on. Your land and your people must someday . . . be free." The strength suddenly faded from Akin's voice as the blood welling from his mouth became thicker and darker. "Free," he whispered again, and then he was gone.

Longarm gently laid Akin's head on the ground and stood up. Some of the other men had gathered around him. They all took off their sombreros and bowed their heads.

"Hey, big brother!" a harsh, mocking voice suddenly called, intruding into the respectful silence.

Longarm whirled around. Several yards away, Jack Ralston stood with his left arm looped tightly around the neck of Silvia Gonzalez. The barrel of the gun in his right hand was pressed against her head just above her right ear. Ralston had positioned himself so that none of the Children of Liberty could fire at him without hitting Silvia.

"You son of a bitch!" Longarm grated. "Let her go!"

"The hell you say, big brother," Ralston said sneeringly. Even in these circumstances, his arrogant self-confidence had not deserted him. "Get me some horses so the girl and I can ride out of here, or I swear I'll put a bullet right through her brain."

Chapter 33

'Ralston!" Sam Horne said sharply. "Blast it, man, you're a Texas Ranger! You can't do this."

"Not any more, Horne," Ralston replied. "I can't ever go back to Texas. Not as long as you and my so-called brother there are still alive." He looked at Longarm. "What is your name anyway?"

Longarm didn't like carrying on a conversation like this while a gun barrel was jabbed painfully against Silvia's head, but he answered Ralston's question. "Custis Long. I'm a United States deputy marshal. And you're right, Ralston. The only thing waiting for you north of the border is a hang-rope."

"Unless," Ralston said with a grin, "I kill you and Horne here. Then there wouldn't be anybody who could prove that I made a deal with Mendoza and then Claudio."

"I would tell," Silvia said between gritted teeth. "I would tell everyone the truth about you!"

"Who'd take the word of a Mexican slut over that of a Texas Ranger?" asked Ralston. "You know, Silvia, my only regret about this whole mess is that I didn't screw you back in Presidio when I had the chance. You were practically panting for it, like a bitch dog in heat."

Stanley's face was dark with rage as Ralston poured out his venom. Horne was furious too. Longarm forced himself to remain cool, though, as he said, "If we let you go, Ralston, what guarantee do we have that you won't hurt Silvia?"

"Why would I hurt her? She's my ticket out of here." Ralston licked his lips and laughed. "I might have a little fun with her before I let her go, though. Teach her what gringo lovin' is all about."

"Too bad," Longarm said softly. "You ain't going anywhere, old son." Slowly, he started to draw his Colt, which he had never had the chance to reload after the flurry of shots in the outlaw camp.

"What the hell!" Ralston exclaimed with sudden confusion showing on his face. He didn't know whether to take a shot at Longarm or keep the gun pressed to Silvia's head.

Ralston's moment of hesitation gave Longarm the chance to point his empty gun at Ralston's head, which was visible past Silvia's shoulder. Ralston crouched a little to make himself a smaller target and shouted nervously, "I'll kill her, I swear I will!"

"And if you pull that trigger, you'll be a dead man yourself a second later," Longarm vowed. He was bluffing, trying to give Silvia a chance to get away from Ralston, but the renegade didn't have to know that. Longarm squinted along the barrel of his Colt. "Because I don't aim to miss."

Ralston's face twisted with hatred as he jerked the barrel of his gun away from Silvia's head and fired at Longarm. Longarm was already moving to the side, though, and the bullet whined harmlessly past his ear.

Before Ralston could move his gun back to its original position, Silvia reached up and grabbed the wrist of his gun hand. She twisted in his grip with surprising strength and sank her teeth into his arm. Ralston yelled in pain and dropped the gun.

No one could shoot because Silvia was still in the way. She hit Ralston in the chest, hard, and broke free of him. Instead of getting away from him, though, she dived for the gun he had dropped and snatched it up as he staggered back a step.

Longarm had seen the speed with which Silvia could move. Her arm was a blur as she brought the gun up and fired. The sharp crack and the accompanying burst of flame and smoke sent Ralston stumbling backward even farther. He pressed his hands to his chest as he tried to keep his feet, but he sat down hard on the ground. He said in a choked voice, "Silvia?" And then blood gouted from his mouth. He fell to the side and didn't move again.

"There," Silvia said as she lowered the gun. "That is what you get from me, bastard."

Longarm holstered his Colt and started toward her, thinking that the reaction from what had just happened might make her collapse when it hit her. Instead, she swung around toward the others with the gun held at her side and began issuing orders in a strong, clear voice.

"Gather up all the guns and horses. The bandits who are still alive will go free, but unarmed and on foot, and if any of them ever come back to these mountains, they are to be killed on sight."

Stanley and the other revolutionaries nodded in understanding.

Longarm smiled slightly. He was starting to see what Silvia's true place in Los Niños de Libertad really was.

Silvia looked down in sorrow at Benjamin Akin's body. "We will bury Benjamin," she said. "The dead bandits can lie where they have fallen."

"Silvia . . ." her brother said hesitantly. "Do not harden your heart too much."

"Sometimes it takes a hard heart to win freedom," Silvia shot back. "There will be time for other things when the people of Mexico breathe the air of liberty."

She had learned a lot from Benjamin Akin, thought Longarm. A hell of a lot.

"What are you going to tell your boss when you get back to Denver?" Sam Horne asked as he and Longarm rode toward the Rio Grande a few days later, leading several packhorses loaded down with long, canvas-wrapped bundles containing the stolen Army rifles.

"That I did my job and got those rifles back," Longarm replied. "What else is there to tell?"

"That you let a bunch of Mexican revolutionaries go on their way with enough loot from that payroll robbery to buy plenty of brand-new Winchesters? That they're going to raise holy hell with Diaz's *rurales* for a long time to come?"

"Is that what you're going to put in your report to Ranger headquarters?" Longarm asked.

"Hell, no! It ain't the Rangers' job to save El Presidente's bacon for him."

"It ain't mine either," said Longarm.

They rode on, and in the distance he saw the line of green that marked the trees along the Rio Grande. In another half hour, they would be back across the border. He would make arrangements to have those rifles freighted to El Paso, where they had been bound for originally, and once they got there, the Army could do whatever they damned well pleased with them. They could melt them down for scrap as far as Longarm was concerned.

He remembered his farewell to Silvia Gonzalez. For a moment, she had let the tough exterior of leadership slip as she came into his arms for a kiss. Her lips had been as warm and sweet-tasting as ever.

"Someday you will come back to Mexico, Custis?" she had whispered to him.

"More than likely," he'd replied, without mentioning that it would probably be his job that brought him there. *Quien sabe?*

Someday he might find himself looking for her, with orders to stop her.

But not today, he told himself as he rode on toward the Rio Grande. If he crossed paths again with Silvia Gonzalez, it would be in the future.

"You know, Long," Sam Horne said slowly, "you ain't such a bad sort. For a federal lawman, that is."

"And you ain't as all-fired stubborn as some Texas Rangers," Longarm replied with a grin.

"Still, I reckon it'd be all right with me if you never showed your face in Presidio again."

Longarm thought about Silvia Gonzalez and said quietly, "Amen to that, old son. Amen to that."

Explore the exciting Old West with one of the men who made it wild!